ONE GIRL, BIG WORLD, HARD DREAM

CAN I DO THIS ALONE

SARAH A. STEED

WESTBOW
PRESS®
A DIVISION OF THOMAS NELSON
& ZONDERVAN

WestBow Press books may be ordered through booksellers or by contacting:

WestBow Press
A Division of Thomas Nelson & Zondervan
1663 Liberty Drive
Bloomington, IN 47403
www.westbowpress.com
1 (866) 928-1240

ISBN: 978-1-5127-4310-4 (sc)
ISBN: 978-1-5127-4311-1 (hc)
ISBN: 978-1-5127-4309-8 (e)

Library of Congress Control Number: 2016908183

Print information available on the last page.

WestBow Press rev. date: 06/13/2016

Contents

CHAPTER 1

"**S**usan, time for dinner!" Mom yelled from the kitchen.

"Coming!" I yelled back.

While I was walking to the kitchen, Dad walked in the door. "Hello, family!"

"Daddy's home!" I screamed.

We walked into the kitchen and sat down. We prayed and then ate for a while in silence. Eventually, I asked, "When do you think Jesus Christ will come back? I have heard the pastor talking about how close it is, with all the earth disasters and this guy Abram coming out of nowhere, rising higher in power almost every day. I mean, it seemed like last week he was nobody, but all of the sudden, he's a big deal."

"Yes, it does seem like it, but God has His timing. We don't know when it's going to happen. Nobody knows except for God, but the Bible says He will come back when you're not thinking about it."

"So He won't come right now?"

"No!"

"Good. There are still things I want to do before I go to heaven."

Mom asked, "Like what, Susan?"

"Go to Paris, go on a date, get married, have my first kiss—the list goes on and on."

"Susan, things are going to be a lot better in heaven." Dad jumped right in. "If you're so curious about the second coming, then why don't we see the new movie *Left Behind*? I hear they remade it."

"That's a great idea, Dad!"

"What about tomorrow?"

"Perfect!"

We took our plates to the sink, and I ran upstairs to get ready for bed. I'm one of those people who like to go to bed early. If I don't get my sleep, I am very grouchy in the mornings.

"Wake up, Susan. Time to go to school!" Mom yelled from the bottom of the stairs.

I got up and put on some blue jeans, my green-striped shirt, and white shoes. I walked downstairs, grabbed a box of Frosted Flakes, and quickly ate. My bus driver comes early because she doesn't want to be late for her bingo club, which starts at eight o'clock. We have to make sure we are at the bus station twenty minutes early. One time I was eight minutes early and missed the bus. She races down the road at seventy-five miles per hour, stopping for three seconds to let ten kids on the bus. Just make sure you make it in time. One kid was very close to the first step when the three seconds were up. She closed the door, and he didn't come to school. I'm surprised she hasn't been reported yet.

I kissed my mom good-bye and climbed onto the speedy Eddie bus. That's what we call our bus. I heard someone yelling for me.

"Susan, Susan, come sit with me," my best friend Natalie said.

We talked about how evil Mrs. Stringer is. That's our Bible teacher. She always gives us bucket loads of homework. I have never really understood her. She is a weird teacher who doesn't like to talk. All she does is write our assignment on the board, and then we turn it in for a grade. It's a simple class but one that's easy to get bored in.

We arrived, and Miss Eddie dumped us off. I walked to my locker and put my stuff up. Then the hip girls walked in.

They walked like VIPs in a movie—all fancy looking, not very smart, high heels, and the boys drool all over themselves when they're around. For tenth graders, they sure do know how to walk the halls; I'll give them that. You can tell their parents are rich. I sometimes wish I was part of that group. People don't seem to notice me, and they make me feel small and unimportant. It's hard for me to make friends. I'm smart, I'm not pretty, and my parents aren't rich. I'm not the total package that kids want. Kids these days buy friends who come with pretty bodies, are popular, have a rich lifestyle, and have no brains. I sometimes wish I came with that kind of package.

Julia walked up to me and slammed my locker shut. "Susan, oh, I'm so glad I ran into you. Can you do me a favor?"

She wants me to do a favor for her? Wow!

"Um, yeah." I was trying to act hip.

"Great. Go buy me a soda out of the teachers' workroom? Here's some money, and you can keep the change."

Really? Go buy yourself a soda. No way. I'm not your maid!

"Sure!" What could I say—*No, I'm not your slave?* I would get hit by her twenty-pound purse if I said that.

While walking to the teachers' workroom, I ran into Natalie. "Hey, Susan, where are you going? Our class is the other way."

"I'm going to get Julia a soda."

"*From the teachers' workroom?*" Natalie screamed.

"Shhh. Keep your voice down!"

"Don't fall for that. I did that last week and got in trouble for going in there. Plus there was no change."

"But if I don't, she will whack me with her huge purse."

"Well, looks like a no-win situation."

"Thanks for the tip, but I have to do this if I want to be noticed by the cool kids."

3

"I'm warning you. If you go in the teachers' workroom and get caught, it will go on your permanent record. Don't you want to go to a good college?"

"Yeah," I said, feeling stupid. I'm also one of those kids who thinks that if you mess up one time, your future is ruined.

"Then don't do it! Come back with me, and let's go to class. This is just Satan talking. Move him away, and let's go."

Thinking about what she said, I wondered what would happen if I didn't go with Natalie. Sometimes I wish I had a what-if machine. What if I didn't listen to her? What would happen? I decided to go with Natalie.

"Okay, but if I come home with a black eye, I blame you."

I opened the door to my house and saw a glowing light; a man stood there. His head and hair were like wool that was as white as snow, and his eyes were like flames of fire. His voice was like the sound of many waters. He spoke to me.

"Don't be afraid. I am the Alpha and Omega, the Beginning and the End, and the First and the Last."

He then disappeared. I ran to the kitchen where Mom was and told her what I had seen. She didn't understand me.

Did that man come for me? Was I the only one who saw?

Many questions ran through my head as I wondered, *Why?*

CHAPTER 2

A t lunchtime the next day, I was zoned out, thinking. Ella, a friend, came and sat next to me with her lunch tray. "Ella, can I ask you a question?"

She nodded yes.

"Have you ever had someone appear and then disappear before your eyes?"

I then told her what I'd seen yesterday when I opened the door to my house.

She didn't understand me either. "Um, that's something that you may want to ask Mrs. Stringer."

I laughed till I almost cried. "You must be joking!"

"No. Maybe Mrs. Stringer would know something about that weird creature you saw."

It all came down to one thing: I had to go with what Ella suggested.

I walked down the long corridor to Mrs. Stringer's classroom. She sat at her desk with her pink glasses, grading papers.

"Hi, Mrs. Stringer. Can I tell you something?"

"Sure," she responded.

"I saw a man yesterday, and he introduced himself to me, but I still didn't know who he was."

She said in a whisper so that I had to lean in to hear her, "What did he tell you?"

"I am the Alpha and Omega, the Beginning and the End, and the First and the Last."

"That's very interesting! John was told the same thing; it was Jesus!"

"So you're saying that Jesus came down from heaven to tell me who He is."

She nodded.

"That doesn't make sense."

"Well, then you need to read Revelation—the whole book."

"Okay, I will. Thanks!"

I walked back up the long corridor to the lunchroom. I sat back down and said to Ella, "You know, Mrs. Stringer is not that bad."

"Says the girl who thought my suggestion was lame."

I went home, did my homework, and then read from the book of Revelation.

When I was on the last chapter, Dad called me to come downstairs. "Ready for the movie, Sue?"

"Oh yeah. I'm ready to get some answers."

"Get in the car, and we'll be on our way."

I was so excited to see the movie. I had read some of Revelation, and it was like a time machine right under my nose. It told of everything that would happen, and I couldn't wait to see it unfold on a big screen.

We reached the movie theater and strolled in.

"Hello," my dad said. "We would like three tickets to *Left Behind*, please."

"I'm sorry. We only have two seats left."

"Um, it's okay. We'll come back another day," Dad said sadly to the ticket-window lady.

"Sorry, Sue. Maybe we can go tomorrow?"

"Okay, that's fine," I said, even though I was disappointed that I couldn't see it today.

So we went back home and got ready for bed. I then read the last chapter of Revelation. I was really confused at first, but I pulled out my church notes, and it made much more sense. It told me that Satan was already defeated after Jesus rose from the dead. John was the only one who got to see what the end would be like. He explained things very well. After I finished reading, I drifted off to sleep.

———————————◁▷———————————

It was Saturday, and I was happy that I didn't have to wake up early. I grabbed my robe and slippers and put them on. I jumped down the steps and zoomed into the kitchen. Dad was sitting at the snack bar reading the *Daily News* on his iPad.

"Good morning, sweetheart! Did you sleep well?"

"Sure!"

"That wasn't a positive 'sure'!"

"I didn't sleep great, and I didn't sleep badly. So I slept okay."

"Okay, what would you like for breakfast?"

"How about those awesome waffles that you make?"

"Sit back, relax, and I will do that!" Dad loves saying that. Some people have their catchphrases, and that's his.

I received my blueberry waffle. It was light and tasty.

"This is great, Dad. Thanks!"

"I would do anything for you, Sue."

"Can we see the movie today?" I asked.

"We can surely try!" he assured me.

Then Mom screamed from across the house. "Sam, get your tail in our room now!"

"I'll be right back! Don't worry. Everything will be just fine." He got up and walked to his room. I had the scary feeling that they were going to argue, so I tiptoed toward their room and heard Mom raising her voice at Dad.

"Now, Sam, I told you not to spend your money on crazy stuff. We have a budget here; we are almost a month behind on paying all of our bills. If we don't have the money in the next ten days we will lose our house or have to put Susan back into a public school. Is that what you want?"

I didn't hear him say no, so I guessed he shook his head. Were we going to lose the house? Mom was a bank teller, and my dad was a shoe salesman. They both had low-paying jobs. What were we going to do? I ran up to our prayer room. It was a small room with a bench and a Bible. I bowed my head and prayed.

"Dear Lord, You are almighty! You gave Your life for us so we could live. Lord, I want to thank You for wonderful parents. They need Your help. You know how much money is in their savings account. Help them get through this. Thank You for being a God who loves and provides for us. Amen!"

"You ready to see this movie?" Dad asked me.

"I guess!"

"What's wrong? Did you hear Mom and me talking?"

"I want to say no, but that would be lying … so, yes!"

"Sue, look at me. We are going to be fine. God will take care of us." I didn't see how Dad can be so calm. I had never seen him get upset. He was like the sun, always shining and never losing energy.

"I know!"

"Then let's go see this movie."

"Three movie tickets for *Left Behind*, please!" Dad said kindly.

"Okay, do you have your Regal card?" Dad gave the woman his card.

"Okay, here are the tickets. Have a great time." We walked inside the theater and handed the tickets to the ticket taker.

"Your movie will be the third door on the left. Hope you enjoy."

I came out of the theater with a new mind. The way God does things is just incredible. The disappearances of kids and some adults were just outstanding in the movie. It was amazing the way their clothes fell in a neat stack on the shoes and how their bodies went to heaven. I hope someone I will be around when everyone disappears to explain what happened. Hmm ...

CHAPTER 3

I t was Monday morning, the first day of the school week. I woke up and asked God, as I did every Monday morning, "What do You want to teach me this week? How can I make a difference in someone's life?" I walked downstairs and got my usual breakfast. Then Mom walked in. I asked her, "What are you doing today?"

"I wish I knew! What are you doing today?"

"Mom, you know what I'm doing today. The same thing I do every Monday."

"Oh yeah, sorry. I guess I'm not completely awake yet."

❧

It was Bible time, which was now my favorite class. Mrs. Stringer walked in, and she wrote on the board, "Get out your Bible, and turn to Isaiah 28:23. Then write your thoughts on a sheet of notebook paper. We will talk after everyone is done."

I turned to Isaiah and read, "Give ear and hear my voice, Listen and hear my speech." I took out a piece of paper and wrote, "When God comes to you, listen and obey Him, for He knows all things. Never underestimate what God tells you. God ..." Before I could finish, I heard the fire alarm. We filed outside, and Mrs. Stringer took roll.

We were outside for the rest of the class. I never did finish what I wrote; I just had to turn it in as it was.

That night Daddy came home early, so we had dinner when I got home from school. We had spicy chicken, mashed potatoes, broccoli, and green beans.

When it was time to go to bed. I prayed that God would leave me here when He came back to take his people with Him so I could teach others about Him. I knew it was a crazy thing to ask, but that's what I wanted to do. I then fell asleep.

I woke up from a dream. It had a yellow glowing golden retriever statue sitting in a corner of a cabin. The owner was a young girl with her father sitting on the couch reading the Bible. They were happy! They wore big smiles on their faces. It's the smile you would find on a TV commercial. Dreams are weird, huh?

I sat down on the bus on the fourth row to the right. I rode all the way to Natalie's house. She got on the bus, and I heard a loud trumpet that sounded like a chorus of hallelujahs. She said, "I need a—"

Poof! She disappeared. I looked over to the bus driver; she too had disappeared. Only their clothes were left. It was just like the movie. I was the only one left on the bus. Was I left alone? And I was riding in a bus without a bus driver. I quickly ran to the steering wheel and hit the brake pedal. The bus stopped in the middle of the road. In the rearview window I saw a car behind the bus driving without a driver. I opened up the door, and just as I jumped out, the car crashed into the bus. The bus was a goner. I got out just in time!

CHAPTER 4

I heard someone calling out, "Susan, is that you?" I turned around and saw Mrs. Erica standing right next to me with red, puffy eyes.

"Mrs. Erica, are you okay?"

"Where's my little Natalie?"

"I'm sorry, but she's gone."

With a loud scream she yelled, "*No*! What happened to her then?" I didn't answer her. I didn't know how to.

"What could have caused this?"

At that moment I knew exactly what happened. I explained the rapture to her, how Jesus came back and took His people with Him. Sadly, she didn't understand a word I said.

I hurried back to my house and fell asleep, hoping this was a dream. My world was empty. No one was there. My parents were gone, but I had to remember that God was still with me.

After I woke up I went to the police department to see if everyone was okay, but I would never do it again. All the prisoners had broken free. There were only two policemen there. One was shot and killed on sight; the other was fighting with all the strength he had in him. While I was walking back to my house, I noticed everything around me was out of control. There were car accidents, fires, people stealing, and people walking with puzzled looks on their faces, wondering what was happening. All around, people were weeping. I finally made it back to my house away from all the chaos that was happening.

———————————— ⟨⟩ ————————————

Ding-dong! I walked over to the door to see who it was. It was Chloe, Ella's mom. I opened the door.

"Hey, Susan. You're the only kid left. Everyone one else is gone," she said

"I am? Wow!"

"Yeah, are your parents here?"

"No, I wish."

"Where are they?"

"They are in heaven with Jesus. Do you believe in Him?" I asked her. She nodded yes. "Then why didn't you give your life over to Him?"

"I never had the time to give my life over to Him."

"Now is the perfect time. So why don't you?"

"I'm not ready yet. Right now I'm just really confused."

"It's okay if you are confused, but things are not going to get any easier. I would suggest doing it really soon," I said.

She turned around, and I walked out with her to check the mail. Guess what was in there? Bills from the phone company, the mortgage company, the electric company, and the water facility. Wow, being a grown-up takes a lot of effort. I decided to go to the bank.

When I got there I saw a lady standing off to the side of the building, weeping. I walked up to her and asked, "Why is the bank so crowed?"

"It's just like the depression. Everyone running to grab all their money before the bank runs out," she replied.

Okay, I guess I should have not been surprised by that, but I had to find a way to get that money. I started crying. How could I find so much money in a short period of time?

CHAPTER 5

A couple of days later …

Ding-dong!

I ran to the door to see who it was. I didn't recognize the face, so I opened the door slowly. "Hello, I'm Rob. I'm here to tell you that you are late paying your bills. You have just two days before I take away your—"

Before he even finished, I slammed the door shut. It was around lunchtime, but I was not hungry. I sat down on the couch sobbing. I wanted my father. Oh, how I wanted his soft arms around me, comforting me. I could just hear his soft, loving voice say, "It's okay, Sue. It's okay! I am right here." Then his voice drifted away.

I decided to watch TV to get my mind off of things. All that was on was some guy called Abram Bloom coming to rule the world. He was explaining that the Wailing Wall had been closed down and the United States needs to sign a peace treaty with Israel. I could not stop thinking about what had happened, so I turned off the TV. Then out of nowhere a glowing light appeared, and the same Man that had visited before stood there.

He said, "Do not be afraid. I am the Alpha and Omega, the Beginning and the End, and the First and the Last. I have come to tell you that you are in the last days of Earth. You will be okay, I promise. I will always be with you and love you. I am the End." Then He disappeared. Now I knew what He meant. Why couldn't He have told me that I would be left behind the first time I saw him?

Two days later …

Ding-dong! I was ready to go. I got my bags and headed for the door. I knew God was going to take care of me. I opened the door, and Rob said in a sad voice, "I am here to take your house. Are you ready?"

I nodded.

"Okay, then, let's get 'er done."

While I was walking out, I looked behind me, and all my memories rushed through my mind like a running river. I was going to miss this house. As I walked out, a glowing light appeared. The Man stood there and said, "Do not be afraid. Go near the river, and you will see a wooden house. A young girl named Maddie and her pappy will be there. Go and teach them about Me."

He disappeared. I walked toward the river, as Jesus had told me to do. I followed along the bank of the river. It was even more horrifying than the city. Sadness was everywhere I looked. A plane had crashed with more than 150 people on board, mommies were trying to find their babies, and cars had crashed into the trees. More than ten people came up to me, asking if I had seen their children. I gave them the same answer: "They are in heaven, sitting at Jesus's throne." None of them believed me. So this was what life was going to be like for the next seven years.

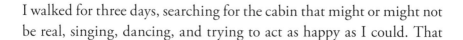

I walked for three days, searching for the cabin that might or might not be real, singing, dancing, and trying to act as happy as I could. That was a challenge. How could someone be happy in a time like this? All I wanted was my mom and dad. My dad used to tell me, "Say what you mean, and mean what you say." So I guess if I had to tell the truth, I was freaking out. I was not singing or dancing, I was acting like a three year old.

"Are we going to be there soon? Are we there yet?"

I kept getting the same answer—no—until the last day. Now I know what Jesus might have felt like. God kept saying no to Jesus coming back to life, until on the third day. I saw a little brown cabin sitting in the distance. It was as still as a mushroom, which is a sign of someone sleeping. Mrs. Stringer taught me that. She said if the house is laughing, then people are having a great time. If the house is loud, then the people are having a party. In this case, the house was sleeping. Now that I thought about it, were there one or more people living in that still cabin? Well, I was going to find out!

I walked up to the cabin and knocked on the door. A young, tall, skinny girl answered. "Hello, have I met you before? You look familiar," she said to me.

"No, I don't think so. Um, are you Maddie?"

"Yes, I am. And who are you?"

"I'm Susan. My house was taken away, and I was sent here for you to take care of me." Not knowing what she would say I scooted away from the door.

"Well then, come on in!" When she let me in, a yellow Golden Retriever was sitting in the right corner. And on the couch was an eighty-five-year-old man sleeping. Everything I saw was in my dream.

CHAPTER 6

She led me to my bedroom. "Wow!" There was clown wallpaper, a clown bedspread, and a huge clown statue in the left corner. "Do I really have to sleep here tonight?" I asked.

"Why, does something bother you?"

"Well, yes, this room is very scary looking."

"Do you want to sleep on the couch instead?"

"That would be lovely." When I got to the couch, the old man was sleeping like a baby. I didn't want to wake him up since he was sleeping so well. "What do I do?" I whispered to Maddie.

"Pappy, Pappy, Pappy, wake up!" Maddie started shaking Pappy.

"Ugh! Why did you wake me up? I was sleeping so well," the man mumbled.

"We have a guest, and she's going to be sleeping on the couch," Maddie told him.

"Why on my good couch?"

"Because she did not like the clown room. So get up!"

"But this is my couch!" he protested

"Pappy!"

Pappy listened to his daughter and went to his room.

"Thank you so much," I said to Maddie.

"No problem! You can stay here for as long as you like."

"Thank you. What are we having for dinner tonight? I'm starving. I've been walking for ages."

"Oh yes, Pappy has to go and catch it."

"What do you mean go and catch it? Is it rabbit, deer, or duck? If it is, I don't like any of those."

"No, no, it's fish!"

"Okay, I love fish."

With a loud scream, Maddie yelled, "Pappy, get up and go catch dinner!"

"Do I have to?" he whined.

"Yes, dear!"

Pappy went out the door with his fishing gear. I guessed Maddie was the "man" of the house. She was always telling her dad what to do. If I had done that to my dad, he would have roared at me, even if he had been eighty-five years old.

I went outside to draw water when I heard a great voice coming from the horizon saying, "Come and see!" And there in the sky was a white horse. The one who sat on it held a bow with no arrows. It was weird, but I do remember reading something from Revelation saying, "And he went out to conquer and to conquer."

"It's the Antichrist!" I screamed. Maddie came running out the door.

"Susan, why are you screaming? Who is it? Whoa! He's beautiful! He's like the savior we have been waiting for. Pappy, come and see!"

"Don't let your eyes deceive you. It's the Devil!" I said.

"Are you crazy? The Devil would be red and evil. How can the Devil be the most beautiful thing you've ever seen? He's more beautiful than the sunrise and sunset and more beautiful than the daisies and roses."

Then when I thought nothing could get worse, Pappy came out. "What did you say, Mad?"

"It's the—"

I interrupted her and said, "It's the Devil!"

"Who did you say it was?" Pappy screamed.

"It is the Devil who has come to destroy this world with war, famine, and death."

Maddie replied, "War and death? You have to be insane or stupid."

"Think what you want, but I warned you!" Then I roamed off.

How could I explain to people that it was the Devil? Could I do this alone? Everywhere I looked, people had their mouths open with amazement. The horse rode all through the earth with a bow. I raced to the cabin, took out my Bible, and turned to Revelation 6:3. I read, "Then he opened the second seal, I heard the second creature saying, 'Come and see.' Another horse fiery red went out. And it was granted to the one who sat on it to take peace from the earth, and that the people should kill one another; and there was given to him a great sword."

I thought, *You mean people are going to run around and kill each other? You have to be kidding me.*

CHAPTER 7

"That was good fish, Mr. … Mr. … um, Mr. Pappy."

"Say thank you, Pappy," Maddie scolded Pappy.

"No, I still don't understand why she's here. Who asked her to come?" Well, that was a little hurtful.

Maddie said, "Susan, dear, why don't you just go take a bath? It's a little brown bucket just outside the door."

I stepped outside and found a brown bucket. I picked it up and put it behind a tree, took off my clothes, and hopped in a bucket the size of a raccoon. How in the world was I going to take a bath in this nasty thing? On the other side was shampoo, conditioner, body wash, and a gray washcloth. The washcloth looked as old as Pappy. I squirted the body wash on the washcloth. Surprisingly, the body wash smelled good. As I washed myself, I thought about my hair. How in the world would I wash my hair in such a small bucket? I looked over at the pond. I hollered from behind the tree, "Maddie, is it okay if I wash my hair in the pond? Also can you bring me a towel?"

"Sure thing. Go ahead." She threw a tablecloth out the window. I got out and ran to the pond naked, hoping no one would see me. I stepped in the shallow end, and it was freezing cold. I went a little deeper when a fish jumped out and slapped me in the face. Now the pond was scarier. It was brown and murky. It was like a kid had taken a bath but never changed the water. I probably stayed in there for five minutes. Well, maybe fifteen. It may have looked gross, but it was magical. When I went underwater, it was blue. It was like water heaven. I got to swim with the fish, but before I got too comfortable, Maddie had to drag me out. When I got out, the shore was already occupied. A big, long copperhead snake slithered over to me and bit right through my toe. The last thing I remembered was falling to the ground. I was out!

———————————————

About three hours later, I was lying on the couch.

"What happened?"

"I had a notion. Pappy!"

"What do you mean, Pappy?" I asked nervously.

"He sucked all the poison out of you."

"Thanks to you, I had to brush my teeth about five times," Pappy scolded me.

Then I heard a great voice coming from the horizon saying, "Come and see!"

When I wobbled outside, there stood in the sky a fiery red horse. The one who sat on it had a great sword. I pulled out my Bible again and read that he came to take away peace and start a war. Next I heard a loud banging on the door. Maddie tiptoed to the door and looked out the peephole. There stood an ugly-looking man with tattoos everywhere, a gun in his hand, and a mad look on his face.

He screamed from the top of his lungs, "Let me in, and I'll kill you!"

"What should I do?" Maddie whispered.

"Let him in!" I uttered.

"What? But he is going to kill us!"

"God will take care of us!" I assured her.

"Sure, trust in a God who does not exist. Maybe we should pray to that savior on the white horse—the one we just saw." She reached and opened the door. The man stomped in and cocked the gun.

"I always keep my word!" The ugly man screamed at us. In his voice you could tell he was drunk.

"Maybe this time you could lie?" I said as he moved closer.

He walked over to me, pointed the gun, and pulled the trigger. I felt peace come over me, and I couldn't move. The earth stopped spinning, and everything slowed down. I saw the bullet pop out of the hole as it hurtled toward me. I froze, not knowing what to do. The bullet bounced right off of me, and it hurtled back toward the creepy man. It was like I was in a bubble that could not be popped. It hit the man, killed him instantly, and the earth started spinning again. Everything went back to normal.

"What just happened?" Maddie asked.

"We just experienced an act of God."

I woke up at five o'clock with pain in my toe. I saw a glowing light. The Man stood there and said, "Well done, Susan. Thanks to you, Mrs. Chloe is a Christian now. She is coming in one minute. Teach Maddie and Pappy about Me. I am the Alpha and Omega, the Beginning and the End, and the First and the Last." Then He disappeared.

Pappy walked into the kitchen, ready to have breakfast. In a deep, dark voice he asked, "Why are you still in my house?"

"I sleep here!"

"Well, I have a fantastical notion—get out!"

Then Maddie came in and yelled, "Stop being so frenzied, you guys!"

"Sorry!" I said.

Ding-dong! Maddie went over to the door.

"I don't know who it is," Maddie whispered.

"Just open it!" Pappy scolded.

When Maddie opened the door, Mrs. Chloe saw me out of the corner of her eye. "Oh hey, Susan. I have been looking for you."

"I will give you some privacy. Come on, Pappy." Maddie started to grab Pappy.

"No, I want to stay and listen." Pappy said.

"But Pappy, come on." He stayed anyway. Maddie left the room.

"Guess what, Susan?" Mrs. Chloe said.

"You are a Christian now?"

"How did you know?"

"A little angel told me."

"Wow, I have been looking for you all night just to tell you my good news."

"Thanks for telling me. Bye!"

Maddie walked from behind the wall and asked, "I couldn't help but overhear. What is a Christian?"

"It's when you believe that Jesus died on the cross and rose from the dead to save you. He took your cross and died on your cross for you—all to just forgive us from our sins. Do you believe in that?"

"Um, I don't know. How do you know? Did you see it happen?"

"No, the reason I know is the Bible. It tells you everything about divorce, fasting, praying, loving your enemies, and much more."

"Do you have a Bible?"

"Yeah, do you want to read it?"

"Do you mind?"

"No, you can always read my Bible. You need to read Revelation, the whole book. It will explain everything."

"Like how everyone disappeared?"

"Yes! Everything that Jesus said is in red."

"Pappy, do you want to join us?"

Pappy replied, "No, I don't see how you believe in that junk."

"Do you have a better notion?" She asked.

"No!" Pappy came and sat down on the couch near Maddie. She began to read the Revelation.

"The Revelation of Jesus Christ, which God gave him to show his people what, must soon take place. Jesus is coming. 'Behold I am coming soon! My reward is with me, and I will give to everyone according to what he has done. I am the Alpha and Omega, the beginning and the end, and the first and the last.'

"Did Jesus come again?"

"Yes! Jesus took His Christians with Him to this place called heaven, where everything is perfect. See, Jesus is the way to heaven. Read John 14:6–7." Maddie flipped to the book of John and began to read.

"'I am the way and the truth and the life. No one comes to the Father except through me. If you really knew me, you would know my Father as well. From now on, you do know him and have seen him.' I don't think I'm ready to become a Christian."

Pappy jumped up. "Well, what a great fairytale. Are you crazy? You believe that someone hundreds of years ago forgave me of my sins before I was even born? That's just weird. And on top of that, you expect me to believe someone died and rose from the dead? Well, no way, I'm not going to believe that." Then he walked away.

Maddie looked up from my Bible and asked, "So where do you go if you don't believe?"

"It's a place called Hell, where your body is always on fire and horrible things will always happen. If you pray to God there, He will not hear you."

"Do you think Pappy will go there?"

"I don't know. Only God knows. But maybe he will learn."

CHAPTER 8

I woke up at 8:40 a.m. and heard Maddie screaming. She came into the living room out of breath and said, "Susan, help me! Pappy is ... Pappy is ..."

"He's what?"

"He's dying. He was shot." She fainted on the couch. I ran into the bedroom, but it was too late. Pappy lay there, still as the night sky. I went over to the bed and put my hand on his heart. I felt no beat. The Bible was right. People can just die in a couple of hours, and they do it when you least expect it. There was something I was more worried about. I had failed God. He told me to tell them about Him, and I failed. Pappy was in Hell because of me. Tears ran down my face. Maddie walked into the room with her eyes red. We sat on the bed stroking Pappy's hand.

Maddie broke the silence and said, "Life will never be the same. And he went to Hell."

"I failed Him," I whispered.

"You what?"

"I failed God."

"How did you fail Him?"

"I was sent here to teach you about Christ. And now Pappy's dead."

"But you did teach him. This morning he sat down with us and listened to you. He may have not understood, but you still completed the quest."

"Maybe you're right; I guess I did complete the quest. So where are we going to bury him?"

"I was thinking by the deer stand. That's his favorite place."

We went outside and dug a spot for Pappy. We placed him in the hole and said a prayer. Maddie took a rock, got one of Pappy's knives, and carved "Frank Mildred, 1932–2016 Rest in peace." Then she got one of Pappy's deer heads, put flowers on the antlers, and placed it near his grave. The guy who was so rude to me was now a guy I loved with all my heart. I would truly miss him.

Maddie went in and started reading the Bible. When I came in, she closed the Bible and stood up.

"Susan, I am ready."

"Great, repeat after me: Dear Lord, I am ready for You to come into my life. I believe that You died on the cross and rose from the dead on the third day to take away my sins. Amen!" Maddie then grabbed my Bible and started reading again.

That night a glowing light appeared, and the Man stood before me. He said, "Well done, Susan. I have another task for you. Go northeast to the next city. I will guide you to a white house where George and Amanda live. They lost their three children in the rapture. The names of their children are Ethan, Jack, and Stella. George is a drug addict, and Amanda is a very kind lady who is abused by her husband. Stay four months, and talk to them as much as you can. This is a rough place to be. Remember, I will be with you."

"Maddie, pack your bags and gather your stuff. We are going on a trip." I yelled at Maddie.

"Where are we going?" Maddie said as she wobbled into the living room.

"Northeast. What city are we going toward?"

"Atlantic City?" Maddie exclaimed.

"Yeah, that's it!"

"No way—my mother was killed there. I told Pappy I would never go back."

"God told me to go there. He will take care of us, don't you worry. Our Father knows best."

"Well, let me think about it."

"No thinking—there is just go!"

"Okay fine, but if I die, it's your fault." She said walking out of the room.

"Think what you want. I'm going with or without you."

Maddie stopped and turned around. "I'm sorry, I just can't go. I promised Pappy. That would bring up too many sad memories."

"Its okay, there's nothing to be sorry about. If God wanted you to go, He would have told you. I'm leaving early tomorrow morning."

"I hope you have a great trip. Please be careful. How long will you be gone?"

"Four months!"

"Four months? My, that is a long time."

"God does things we may never understand."

"For a fifteen-year-old girl, you're smart."

"God gave me that gift."

"I love how you use God in almost all your sentences."

"Why, thank you!"

"Again, please be careful. The horse brought war. Men are killing men. You're the only one I have left. If I lose you too, I don't know what I will do."

"Don't worry; God is still here with me." Then she hugged me tightly.

CHAPTER 9

Before I left, I turned on the news, and the announcer said that 928,000 men had already been killed.

"Maddie, come look at this." Maddie came in, half awake.

"Oh my, nine hundred twenty-eight thousand men dead."

"Pappy was one of those men."

The TV went red, and the announcer switched gears. "Breaking news! We just got word that Abram Bloom has accepted the position as ruler over the whole world. What a man. Who would have thought? This is the best man the world has ever seen."

Maddie turned it off. "I can't believe I was one of those people who believed he was amazing. By the way, why were you not taken to heaven? Why are you still here?"

"Funny story—I asked God to stay."

"You asked God to do what?" Maddie asked with an open mouth.

"I asked Him, if I was still alive when the rapture happened, if I could stay behind."

"Why in the Sam Hill did you ask that?"

"Somebody had to tell these people what was going on, just like I told you. If I had not asked Him to stay, you would be in Hell. It's common sense. Now I have to get on the road. I have another quest."

"Bye. I will be lonely without you."

"You be careful."

"I will!"

"I'll see you in four months!" Then I walked out the door and headed toward Atlantic City. I was on the way to spread the gospel. Now I know how the disciples felt when they went out to tell people about Jesus.

I spent the night on a park bench in the middle of war, but I still had my bubble of protection around me. Men with guns would come up and shoot me. The bullets bounced off and hit them. I felt safe and comforted in God's arms.

I woke up listening to the sound of death. Have you heard it? You don't want to. It sounded like shouting a deer as it whined before it died. How sad. People left and right were being checked into Hell Eternity Hotel. People died everywhere I went. Blood filled the streets, like the Nile River in Moses's days. There were mothers and fathers crying over the loss of friends and family. Chaos overwhelmed the world.

It was about midmorning when I arrived. There sat a white, loud house, with screaming coming from every window. I thought only two people lived there.

I walked up to the front door and rang the doorbell. I waited and waited, but no one answered. I banged on the door. I shouted, "Is anyone home?" Still no answer. I knew someone was there. I started to walk away when I heard in a soft whisper, "You may come in. Don't be afraid. He won't hurt you." I walked back up and opened the door.

"Hello, is anyone here?"

"Yes, please come upstairs," someone called in a soft voice. I raced upstairs and found a buff man with a bruised woman.

"You must be Amanda and George."

"Why yes—you know our names." The bruised lady said in a quiet voice.

"How do you do?" I asked her.

"Why I'm not doing …" Then George slapped her right across the face. She answered again, "I'm doing great."

"No, you're not."

"What did you say?" George walked right up to my face.

"I said she is not doing great."

"If you want something, now would be the time to ask."

"I would like a place to stay."

"Try next door—they aren't home and will never be home. They're gone, in Hell!"

"Why Hell?" I asked him.

"Satan took up the bad people and left the rest to die on earth."

"That makes no sense."

In a loud scream George said, "If it makes sense to me, then it's true!"

"That's …" I trailed off and said no more. I knew George would hit me if I continued talking. Amanda grabbed my arm and kindly showed me to my room.

"You can stay here for a little bit but not long. George will get mad if you stay too long."

"Why will he be mad?"

"A small girl like you won't understand."

"I can handle it."

"What is your name?"

"Susan!"

"Well, Susan, lunch will be ready in a little bit." I unpacked my stuff and put it away. I knew I was going to stay for four months.

I smelled a hint of smoke, and then it grew stronger and stronger, until I started coughing like crazy. I went downstairs and saw George smoking a Camel on the couch watching *South Park*. I'd heard of it, and Mom told me if I ever watched it, she would punish me severely. George was going to be hard to live with. How did sweet Amanda end up with a horrible man like George?

"Lunch is ready!" I heard from the kitchen.

"I'll be right there after this episode is over." George screamed from the living room.

"How long will that be?"

"You don't need to know."

I jumped right in. "Well, we're eating with or without you."

"You said what?" He put down his cigarette and looked over to me.

"You heard me. Now, Amanda, where are the plates?"

"I put them on the counter."

"Well then, let's start digging in."

"Wait for me!" George screamed. He threw his cigarette in the ash tray and ran to the kitchen. I knew he would come along. I just had to push him.

While we were in the middle of eating, the doorbell rang.

"I'll get it." Amanda said. She walked to the door and opened it.

"I'm Ryan, your neighbor's son. I was wondering if you've seen them."

"I'm sorry, but they disappeared."

"I knew it!"

"You knew what?"

"Got to go."

She closed the door and sat back down. "That Ryan kid knew what happened with the people who disappeared."

George blurted out with mouth full, "I already told you what happened. Why are you so confused? You know sometimes I just want to flick you on the head."

"That was rude," I said without thinking.

"I have said a lot worse."

Without a doubt!

CHAPTER 10

T hen I heard a great voice coming from the horizon, saying, "Come and see!" And there in the sky was a black horse, and the one who sat on it held a pair of scales. Then I heard Amanda scream from the window, "My garden—it just died! Everything is dead. How could it be?"

I ran to look out the window, and the garden had gone brown in an instant. I whispered, "The third horse."

"What happened to my garden? If that garden dies, we won't have any food." Amanda said.

George scolded, "Why not just buy some?"

"It's not that easy. None of us have money." Amanda was getting really upset. She had a beautiful garden. Her whole backyard had been bright green, and now it was brown. She had probably spent years trying to get the garden beautiful.

"Amanda, can you get a beer out of the fridge?"

"This can't be real. Mom warned me about this," Amanda said louder.

"Amanda, did you hear me?"

Oh, how I hated the way George treated his wife. I yelled at him, "She's busy! Don't you get it? You may not have dinner right in front of you for the next seven years. So just shut up! We are living in a time of death and suffering. Don't you care about anybody but yourself? This world was not made for you only. If I were you, I would shut your mouth and start thinking about others. Do I make myself clear?"

"A fifteen-year-old girl telling me what is best for me?"

"No, God is telling you what to do."

"Did you say God?" He was already out of his seat and walking toward me.

"I did! He knows what's best for you."

"I know!"

"You Do?"

"I'm going to heaven. I got saved when I was eight, and when you get saved, you are forever saved. I can do anything I want, and God will forgive me, and then I can start all over again."

"Look at yourself. Do you really think God will let you into heaven? You smoke, you drink, you hit your wife, and you're selfish. Would God want you in heaven if you do all that? And I bet the list goes on. I've just met you, and I know you're going to Hell." George raced up the stairs. I looked over to Amanda, and she was crying like a baby.

"What did you say about your mom being right?" I asked.

"I grew up in church and didn't believe in God. Everyone told me He was real. I just didn't see it. Later I met George in college. He was cute. He hung out with the wrong type of people, but I still loved him. I thought if God was real, then why were so many people still doing wrong stuff? He asked me out, and we went out on several dates. Mom warned me that he was bad. I didn't believe her. Then on my twenty-second birthday, we got engaged. One year later we got married on my twenty-third birthday. We went to Hawaii for our honeymoon. I lived the dream, and then about two years into our marriage, he got bored with me. He started drinking more, and he went out with other women. We had three children. He never was home with me to take care of them. He was never the father I wanted him to be. He broke my heart into pieces. I had it all, but it didn't seem right. I felt like nobody loved me. I never saw my mother after I married. She told me she didn't want to see me. She died two years ago, along with my father. They both had cancer. It was like a sad book, one bad event after another. And after all that, I'm still so miserable. I need a Savior. Susan, who is our Savior? Where can I find Him? Will He love me? Will He watch over me?"

"I have brought good news. Jesus is our Savior. He's right here, surrounding us with His presence. He loves you, no matter what you do. He loves all of us the same—no more, no less. And He was always watching you."

"You mean He was always watching over me?"

"That's right." She got up and left the room. I waited for her to come back, but she didn't.

"Crops all over the world are gone. People, stock up on food; we may not get some for a while. Abram has this under control. He has called on jobs for farming. Anyone interested please call 776-666-9457. Jobs start November 14."

Then I turned off the TV and saw Amanda walking down the stairs.

"Sorry I walked off. I was trying to find my Bible, but I think George threw it away."

"It's fine. You can use mine." I pulled my Bible out of my bag and handed it to her.

"There's one verse I remember from when I was little." She opened the Bible and flipped to Isaiah 41:13: "For I, the Lord your God, will hold your right hand, Saying to you Fear not, I will help you."

"You still remember that?"

"How could I forget? My mom read that verse to me every night when I was scared and not doing well. I felt a connection with that verse, but I kept turning it away. It's amazing what Satan can do. He can make you think one word, and that one word changes your life forever. If I could go back and change everything, I would." Tears started rolling down her cheeks. "I grew up in church. How did I turn away so fast? When I think about my past I—"

"Amanda, get in here and fix the TV!" George screamed.

"When I think about my past, I see Satan's mind. He was turning me in the direction of Hell. And I never knew it."

She got up and wobbled to their room, where George was. I was thinking of how blessed I had been with a good family. I never knew the world could make me hurt over someone else. We get to thinking that our lives are bad, but there are other people who are struggling much more. As I looked at this broken family, I could see hurt and pain all over their faces.

CHAPTER 11

I spent the first night in Stella's bed. It was not comfortable. I felt like I was sleeping on nails. It was rough, and the sheets were very thin. I got very cold. These last couple of days I'd felt homesick. I wanted to sleep in my own bed. I wished I had a fold-up bed I could take wherever I went. That would be cool!

Amanda went over to her neighbor's house and got some eggs from their fridge. She scrambled the eggs for breakfast. I had to hand it to her—she knew how to cook. They were the best eggs in the world.

Amanda started to let her feelings out at breakfast.

"Okay, George, we need to talk," she said in a very serious tone. "I have been thinking about it, and I have made up my mind. I'm sick and tired of you beating and bossing me around. I'm kicking you out of the house. Sorry, you're on your own."

Food dropped from George's mouth. "You can't do that. I am your husband, the one you love, the one you married, the one who gave you children, and the one—"

"Who is packing your stuff and getting out." This was like watching a movie. Screaming, fighting, but would it end happily ever after?

"You are the worst wife ever. Who would kick George Phillip out of his house?"

"Amanda Macon. That's who! I said get out." George jumped out of his seat and ran out the door. I was stunned.

"Ahh, that felt good."

"He left without packing." I reminded her.

"He'll be back when he needs fresh underwear."

Amanda went all through the house, throwing away pictures and any memories of George. She even deleted his Netflix account and tossed out the beer in the fridge. I have never seen someone clean out a house as fast as Amanda. She was running around the house mumbling, "That reminds me of him, so I need to throw it away."

Amanda was right. George came back for his clothes and then left Amanda's life forever. She was happy; she was bouncing off the walls. Then night came, and we found George asleep on the front porch. Amanda wanted to wake him and get him to leave, but I told her to let him sleep. So, we went to bed.

I woke up in the middle of the night and heard, "Come and see." I looked out the window and saw a pale horse with Hades following him. His job was to kill. I ran downstairs and found George dead on the porch. The horse flew off with Hades, taking his soul to Hell. Now George is getting the feel of Hell. Oh, how I wish people would understand that you have to be truly saved to go to heaven. If you think you're saved and live in sin, then you're not saved. When you are saved and you do sin, you feel bad and repent from it. If you're not truly saved and you sin, you don't feel guilty. I wish people would understand that. I hate seeing people who think they are saved go to Hell. Just like George—he said he got saved and lived in sin, but he never felt guilty.

I went back inside and fell asleep. I would tell Amanda in the morning.

I told Amanda. She wasn't that sad. She just continued scrambling eggs. I asked if I could bury George in the backyard, and Amanda said to try somewhere else. I knew she was mad at him, but at least she could be kind enough to bury him in the yard. I buried him in the backyard anyway.

I had some extra cash in my bag, and Amanda and I zoomed to Trader Joe's to get bread. We parked and started to walk in when we heard glass shattering. We looked behind us and saw someone driving Amanda's car. She ran back and yelled for him to stop. Of course he didn't stop, so after we got our bread, we had to walk back home. It took us what felt like years to get home. We were exhausted. Our legs felt like noodles. Amanda flopped on the couch and took a three-hour nap. She slept like a baby.

We had toasted bread for dinner. It wasn't much, but at least it was food. Toward the end of dinner, the doorbell rang. Amanda got up and opened the door. Ryan, their neighbor's son, was there. He was cut, battered, and bruised.

"Oh my, Ryan, what happened to you? Are you okay?"

"I'm fine; I was jumped by a big gang that came out of nowhere. I was hoping you had an extra bed. I'm sorry for showing up like this. I would have called you, but the lines are down."

"Oh yes, we have two extra beds. How did you get here?"

"Crawled. I got jumped right down the road." He fell, and Amanda caught him.

"You come with me, and we'll get you in bed. Susan, dear, can you get some bandages?"

"Yes sure!"

I got up and looked in every cabinet. I couldn't find them. I tried the bathroom, the living room, and every secret compartment. When I opened my mouth to tell Amanda I couldn't find them, an angel appeared. The figure came in a flash and said, "I have come to tell you that Maddie is in heaven with us. Do not cry; you will see her soon." Then as quickly as the angel appeared, she disappeared. I started to weep. I ran to my bed and cried my eyes out. I never got to tell her that she was my best friend. I wonder what the angel meant about me seeing her soon. Maybe she meant in seven years. I cried all the way to Ryan's room and told Amanda what happened. Ryan closed his eyes and fell asleep. Amanda told me to finish my dinner. I walked slowly downstairs and made my way to the kitchen. My eyes were so puffy red that my head started hurting. I skipped the kitchen and headed for the couch and closed my eyes.

It was 7:00 when I awoke. I quietly went upstairs and slowly opened Ryan's door.

"You can come in," said a broken man lying in a bed full of nails.

"I was just making sure you're okay." I walked over to the bed.

"I'm fine, thanks." He sat up, grabbed my hand, and said, "Please stay a little longer. I hear you're a Christian. Is that true?"

"Why, yes. Do you know about our Savior?"

"I wish I did."

"Do you want to know?"

"Yes, please."

"A long time ago, Mary gave birth to Jesus. Jesus is God because God is three in one. Jesus is perfect. He never messed up, and He never sinned. He was and still is almighty. One day He was hung on a cross and died for doing nothing wrong. Three days later He rose again to show that He could not be killed. In forty days, He ascended to heaven. When all those people disappeared, He came back. He took His people with Him, those who truly asked Him into their hearts."

"Then why are you still here?"

"I get that a lot. I asked God to stay behind."

"You're one brave lady."

My cheeks got red.

"So let me get this straight, Jesus died on the cross to save us and to forgive us of our sin?"

"Yes, He loves you so much that He died for you."

"How do you get saved?"

"It's in the Bible." I got out my Bible and gave it to him, and I left the room.

I peeked in about ten minutes later and saw him praying. It just warmed my heart. I loved seeing people get saved.

"You will be changed forever," I whispered and walked off.

CHAPTER 12

"This is Fox Six News. We have breaking news. A fourth of the earth's population is dead. Abram has assured us that due to these deaths, we will now have enough food to feed the world. We are so proud of him for helping us. The world could not ask for a better leader."

"Wow, can you believe this?" Amanda asked me as we watched Fox 6 on the couch.

"Yes, I can believe it. God said it would happen. Is it done? No, we still have more to come." I asked myself, *When will the next seal be opened?*

The ground began to shake, and the sky was rolled away. The altar of God appeared, and men and women stood under the altar. One by one they filed out in a straight line. People started rushing out of their houses to see. They cried out, "How long, O Lord, holy and true, until you judge and avenge our blood on those who dwell on the earth?" Then they all received a white robe and disappeared, and the sky was rolled back into its place. Everyone returned to their duty and asked no questions.

I went back into the house, and Amanda came to me and asked, "Susan, when can I become a child of God?"

"Whenever you think the time is right."

"Well then, the time has come." I ran to get my Bible and turned to Mark 16:16 and read aloud, "He who believes and is baptized will be saved, but he who does not believe will be condemned."

"I just pray the sinner's prayer, right?"

"That's all it takes." Amanda bowed her head and prayed the sinner's prayer. I was so happy I could not stop smiling.

When she was done, we went to a public pool, and I baptized her. I knew I wasn't a pastor, but who else was going to do it? This had truly been a wonderful time, even though I was in the darkest of days. Satan can make it look so bad, but I could still taste and see that the Lord was good. Even in the rough times, there were still people smiling. That makes me remember the song, "Here I Am to Worship":

> Light of the world,
> You stepped down into darkness,
> Opened my eyes let me see.
> Beauty that made,
> This heart adore you,
> Hope of a life spent with you.

I loved to listen to that song every Sunday morning while getting ready for church. It was a good song to start off my day for church. This day was a Sunday, and even if I was not getting ready for church, I still had that song in my heart.

Our dinner was carrots and peas. Amanda had some left over in the fridge. For the first time, Ryan came and joined us.

"Hey, do you have an extra seat for me?" Ryan asked as he struggled to get down the stairs.

"Of course I do—right this way." Amanda showed him where to sit down, and he ate.

"Did you hear that a fourth of the earth's population is dead?" Ryan blurted out.

"How did you find out?" I asked Ryan.

"For a very short time, I was able to get Yahoo News on my phone."

"What else did you find out?"

"Abram is getting ready for the whole world to go to Euros. That means we need to start finding out how to use them." I had to say something, so before Amanda spoke, I did.

"What do we need to buy? No one can grow food, our cars are gone, and we have nowhere to go. I don't see any need to switch to a different currency if we only have seven years left on the earth—if we can even survive till then."

"I have to agree with Susan; we have no need to buy anything." Amanda told Ryan.

"Okay, whatever floats your boat."

Amanda sat up straight, looked confused, and asked, "Where have I heard that?"

"Heard what?"

"Whatever floats your boat."

"A TV show maybe? That's where I learned it."

"No, someone a long time ago used to say that to me when I was little. He would joke around with me when he said it. Oh, how I wish I could remember who it was."

"Was it your dad?"

"No, my dad had another catchphrase."

"Was it a friend?"

"A friend, yeah—that's who it was. Charles! He was my very best friend up until college. I met him when I was in pre-K. But when I met George, well, everything changed. After I went on my first date with him, Charles never spoke to me again. I have never had a closer friend than him. He knew everything about me; he could have been my husband if I would have never met George. I loved him, and he loved me. And that was his catchphrase—'Whatever floats your boat.'"

"I'm so sorry about that. I shouldn't have said anything."

"No, it's not your fault. It's just, I can't believe I couldn't remember him. I often wonder how he is."

"Then why don't you call him?"

"He's probably gone."

"It can't hurt to try."

"Then what are you waiting for?" I stood up and put us back into reality.

"We have no cell service." Amanda turned around and walked slowly back to her chair with her head down.

"I guess you're right."

Ryan jumped right in and said, "You have a landline?"

"Yeah, it's in my bedroom."

"Then why not use that?" Amanda ran upstairs as fast as light traveled. We followed her. She got out her phone book and looked up his name, then dialed his number. We went back down to the kitchen to wait for her so she could have some privacy.

About an hour later, she came back down.

"Well, that took long enough," Ryan said.

"I was so glad to hear his voice again."

"So what did he say?"

"Okay, I'll start back from the very beginning in high school. After he saw me with George, his heart broke. He was so in love with me, that he never dated another woman. I invited him to my wedding, but he never came. The way he described his heart was like someone stomped on it and hit it against the wall several times. He went off on his own and could not stop thinking about me. He was thinking about how happy I probably was—but that's not how it happened, as you know. So he got a job as a family therapist, one of the lowest-paying jobs with a college degree. He was not happy until he spoke to me today. He proposed, so he's coming over tomorrow, and we're getting married. Susan, I want you to be our pastor, and Ryan, would you be our best man?"

"It would be our honor," we said together.

CHAPTER 13

Amanda made herself a wedding dress out of white fabric. We decorated the backyard, and I got my speech ready. I watched all the wedding scenes in movies just to see what the pastor said. They pretty much said the same thing.

Amanda also made a dress for me. Ryan went to his mother's house and got rings from her jewelry box. Charles was able to wear a suit that he found in his closet.

It started around four o'clock.

"We are joined here today to share with Amanda and Charles an important moment in their lives. They were childhood friends who grew apart and are now deciding to live out the rest of their lives as one. Charles, repeat after me. 'Amanda, I take you, to be my wife, my friend, my faithful partner, and my love from this day forward. In the presence of God, who created man and woman to be together, I offer you my solemn vow to be your faithful partner in sickness and in health, in good times and in bad, and in joy as well as in sorrow. I promise to love you unconditionally, to support you in your goals, to honor and respect you, to laugh with you and cry with you, and to cherish you for as long as we both shall live.' Amanda, do you take Charles as your beloved husband?"

"I do!"

"Ryan, can I please see the rings?"

"I, Charles, give you this ring as an eternal symbol of my love and commitment to you." Charles said to Amanda.

"I, Amanda, give you this ring as an eternal symbol of my love and commitment to you." Amanda said to Charles.

"By the power vested in me by our Lord and Savior, God, I now pronounce you husband and wife. You may now kiss the bride."

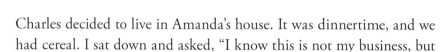

Charles decided to live in Amanda's house. It was dinnertime, and we had cereal. I sat down and asked, "I know this is not my business, but what do you believe in?" I asked Charles.

"I believed the same thing that Amanda did, and I still do."

"Who made you?" I started questioning him.

"My mother and father."

"Who made this wonderful world you live in?"

"Science!"

"Okay, where are you going when you die?"

"The same place you're going—the ground."

"Do you think that's all? That's all there is to life?"

"Yeah, pretty much!"

Amanda jumped right in and said, "Okay, you know what? Why don't we clean the dishes?"

We got up and set our dish in the sink. Ryan went upstairs to lie down, Charles helped Amanda with the dishes, and I went outside to pray.

I stepped out the door and found a gray sky filled with blood—the blood of the souls that died. I wandered over to the sidewalk and bowed my head.

"Dear Lord, I have been blessed with this wonderful family who has been changed by You. Lord, there is one soul who has not been changed. Give me the strength and guidance to know what to say. Thank you for taking care of me through these rough times. Lord, please continue to bless me all the days of my life. Amen!"

I looked up and saw a young lady who was clean. She touched my head, and I felt comforted. She whispered in my ear, "The Lord is my strength and my shield; my heart trusted in him, and I am helped; therefore my heart greatly rejoices, and with him my song I will praise him. God will be with you!" She walked up and disappeared in the sky. I walked back to the house and told everyone goodnight. I would share the good news in the morning. I needed a good, restful night's sleep.

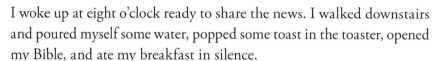

I woke up at eight o'clock ready to share the news. I walked downstairs and poured myself some water, popped some toast in the toaster, opened my Bible, and ate my breakfast in silence.

Amanda came down and told me, "Charles went to Israel to start the new planting job."

"It's not going to help. The crops will just die." I told her.

"Well, we need the money."

"How long will he be gone?"

"As long as they need him."

"No! Aww, man!"

"What?"

"I was …"

"You were going to share the gospel with him."

"Did you hear me outside?"

"No, you've lived with me for a while. I know you. Sorry though!"

"It's fine—God has it all planned out."

"He sure does!"

CHAPTER 14

Amanda and I heard footsteps coming down the stairs. We both turned around and saw Ryan with his bags. He came over to us and gave us a hug.

"It was great being here. Thank you, Amanda, for your hospitality, and thank you, Susan, for telling me about Jesus."

"Where are you going?" Amanda asked with red eyes.

"I'm off. I'm ready to get back on my feet."

"Where will you go?"

"Back home!"

"Without a car?"

"I'll find a way."

"Well, good luck!" I stood up and ran to hug him. "Be careful—this is a very scary time we are living in. Anything can happen."

"I know!" We gave our good-bye hugs, and he walked out of our lives forever.

———

The ground began to shake. It shook the whole world. The earth's crust was crushed open. Everyone ran toward the mountains. Buildings crashed, police cars were everywhere, and firefighters raced on what was left of the road. I grabbed my stuff and headed toward the door when the roof started cracking. Amanda was upstairs, getting her possessions together.

"Amanda, hurry up! The ceiling is about to fall!" I screamed.

"I'm on my way!" I was already outside when the whole house fell to the ground in an instant.

"Amanda, noooo!"

I raced to the house. I rummaged through everything trying to find Amanda. I found a slipper. I traced the slipper up her leg, to her hips, past her chest, and I got to her face. I carried her out of the rubble and onto the grass. I looked at her torn-up face and saw her dancing in heaven with Jesus. She was holding her old Bible. She must have found it after all. I flipped it open and found a note inside from her mother.

> My dearest Amanda,
>
> I hope this Bible gives you what you're looking for. I bought you this Bible many years ago, and I finally had the courage to give it to you. I know this is not what you want, but I hope and pray that you will study it. I have treated you wrongly, and I'm sorry. I hope to see you soon.
>
> With love,
> Your mama

Under that Amanda had written back.

> Oh, Mama, why did you have to leave me so soon? Why, Mama, why? I'm sorry for the way I treated you. I have found the hope to read this. Thanks to my new friend, I have found what I was looking for. Thank you, Mama! I love you always!
>
> With love,
> Your dearest Amanda

I closed it, putting it back safely in her arms, and walked away. I walked for miles until the sun turned black. No one could see. But out came the moon—the red, bloody moon. The whole world turned red from its reflection. Death was near for anyone who did not trust in the name of Jesus Christ. I tried so hard to find my way to the mountain. I read that everyone would run and hide in a cave in the rocks. So I did! Then lights started heading toward the earth. Big and bright lights crashed down to earth. Wildfires spread all across the world. Everything was burned to the ground. I bowed my head and prayed my way to the cave. I made it just before the sky was rolled back like a scroll, and I could see the door gate to heaven. Everyone came out of the cave to look, and they were asking about what was behind the sky. I got on top of a rock and spoke out.

"Everyone, do not be alarmed. This is expected. The Bible told you it was going to happen. Anyone who believes in the name of Jesus Christ will be saved. You are left by God. This is your second chance to trust in His name."

One guy stepped forward and pronounced, "I did believe in His name. But I'm still here."

Another person stepped up and said, "I also believed in His name. I lived my life according to God's Word."

God gave me an overwhelming motivation to share the real truth.

"You are all here today to be given a second chance for God. You missed the boat. God has already come, but He can still come into your lives. Many of you know who He is, and many of you have heard His name once or twice. I don't know your life stories, but somewhere in your lives you have heard the name of Jesus. You can't say that you haven't. Some of you are questioning why you are still here. I have the answer! The answer that all of you are looking for." Many were walking outside.

"Where are you going? It's a mess out there. You have to stay! Anyway, the answer is that you have to truly commit your life to Jesus. Hand over your life to Jesus. Give everything to God. Repent of your sins, and say the sinner's prayer. It's not about how good you are. He doesn't judge you by our standards; He judges you by His standards. Believe me, His ways are higher then ours. What He calls lust is adultery, and what He calls hatred is murder. Everyone has broken a commandment, and everyone can be forgiven. But you need to ask Him to forgive you." Some people started coming up to the front to pray. Many stood behind with evil eyes, but I didn't care. At least some souls were being saved.

Once more the seal was being broken. The mountain was giving its spot up for the Lord. It was removed from its place, along with the islands. Rocks were crumbling, stones were smashing to the ground, and men and women were screaming inside the caves. Many ran out to die. They couldn't take it any longer.

Then the unbelievers started saying to God, "Fall on us and hide us from the face of Him who sits on the throne and from the wrath of the Lamb! For the great day of His wrath has come, and who is able to stand?"

CHAPTER 15

When all the chaos was over, I was lost, not knowing where I would go next. I knelt down on my knees and prayed for God to guide me to where I needed to be. He told me to go to the homeless shelter. I walked for miles, not knowing where I was going. But I was going somewhere—the place that God was leading me to.

I finally came upon an old, rundown building with windows missing, bricks missing, and gang signs written on the walls. I slightly opened the door to voices coming from mad men.

"Hello?" I asked nicely.

A creepy woman in her thirties showed up with missing teeth.

"What do you want? We have no room for you."

"I don't want room. I want people."

"People? What kind of people? We have strong people, old people, mean people, poor people, and boring people."

"I want everyone."

"Everyone? What group do you fall under?"

"The Christian group!"

"Ahh, I see what this is all about. You are one of those crazy people."

"You're right! I am crazy—crazy about God."

"Okay, why don't you run along then, and get lost."

"Just to let you know, I am lost!"

"Well then, stay lost!" she screamed and slammed the door in my face. I tramped off to a bench and spent the night. Listening and obeying God is a lot harder than it seems.

I woke up to a blind man in front of me. I sat up, and he sat down right next to me. He was a small man with gray hair, a curvy face, and a T-shirt with the words, "Seven angels and seven trumpets beware."

"Hello, you lost?" the man asked me and looked straight at me.

"No, I'm found!" I told him, very confused. How did he know I was sitting here? Why did he wait for me to move? How did he know I might be lost?

"You seem confused, my child." How did he know that?

"I am confused. Not about what's happening, but about you."

"There is nothing to be confused at."

"Then why are you blind?"

"Oh my child, you should know."

"But I don't know."

"I'm blind in my faith, not really blind in sight. I could see the mountains move, and I could see the horses plain as day."

"What happened?"

He looked up to the heavens and said, "I found myself in a pit—a pit far away from God. I told Him there was nothing that could change my mind about Him."

"Change your mind about what?"

"You see, I read the Bible cover to cover, knew everything about it. I could quote Psalm 119. But my faith was fake. He took my wife, three children, mother, father, and unborn child in an earthquake. My wife was four weeks pregnant, and they died together in a building that collapsed right on them. I was upset at God for all He took away from me. So I told Him He was not real, not a god, not anything, and I never picked up the Bible ever again. Then I turned blind. I missed everything that was happening all because I was blind. My child, I didn't see the rapture happen. I was too worried about myself. I didn't notice anybody else. That's how blind I was. I threw my whole life away and gave it to Satan, and I'm sitting here now thinking how stupid that was. All my life I read the Bible, I went to church, and I studied His Word every night. It was still all to fake. But look how I turned out—a homeless, old man buried in sin."

"How long ago was the earthquake?"

"Thirty years ago."

"How old are you?"

"I'm seventy-five."

"How did you figure out all this?"

"Again, I read the whole Bible; I knew this was going to happen. I found this shirt in the back of my closet and finally had the heart to wear it."

"Have you repented of your sins?"

"Yes, ma'am, I did!"

"So, what are you looking for?"

"I'm looking for hope." I pulled open my bag and grabbed my extra Bible and handed to him.

"No, I can't take your Bible."

"It's an extra. Take it!" He took it and read Psalm 119. "It's been a while since I've read this, but I still remember." He stood up and walked away and came back with a bag.

"Here, reach into the bag and take it!" At first I was scared, but I reached into the bag and pulled out a watch—a pretty, silver, sparkly watch. I stared at him.

"That was my wife's watch; she wore it all the time. But when she died I found this on the back of her watch."

W—walk

A—above

T—the

C—Christ's

H—hand

"What does that mean?"

"'Walk above the Christ's hand' means God will catch you in His hands if you fall."

"Thank you!" I put it on my wrist.

"Do you have a place to stay?" I shook my head no. "Well, then, you can stay with me."

"It didn't fall in the earthquake?"

"Maybe it was meant to be that way."

"I never asked you what your name is."

"John! Yours?"

"Susan!"

CHAPTER 16

John led me to a small house on the lake that looked like it had been washed over many times. It looked like the house of Charlie Bucket from *Charlie and the Chocolate Factory*. When I entered, I saw a pillow and newspaper. There was a fire going and a cooler right next to the bed. The bathroom was a little pit right outside the house.

"Well, what do you think?"

"It's something!"

"Yeah, I'm sorry, my house got knocked down by another earthquake. I was blessed enough to recover a cooler."

"Well, it's better than living in a homeless shelter."

"I wouldn't say that. They have running water."

"You have a lake."

"They have food on their plate every night."

"You have fish that swim in the lake. You also have deer and squirrels."

"They have a place to sleep with real blankets."

"You have the green grass that God made for man to sleep on."

"They have—"

"You have everything you need right here. Be proud that you have a roof over your head, ground to sleep on, food to eat, and a Bible to read."

"You're right. Why am I complaining when I have everything I need?"

"So, where am I going sleep tonight?"

"Right next to me, if that's okay."

"But I don't know you!" I protested.

"That's okay," he said. With that remark, I felt a little uncomfortable.

"I'll sleep outside!"

"No, you don't have to do that."

"It's my choice." And we left it at that.

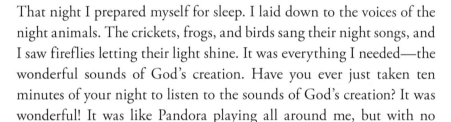

That night I prepared myself for sleep. I laid down to the voices of the night animals. The crickets, frogs, and birds sang their night songs, and I saw fireflies letting their light shine. It was everything I needed—the wonderful sounds of God's creation. Have you ever just taken ten minutes of your night to listen to the sounds of God's creation? It was wonderful! It was like Pandora playing all around me, but with no commercials. It made me remember all of the glorious things that God made. Everything was perfect for a little while.

John woke me up bright and early.

"Come on, we have to get breakfast."

"What is it?" I had clearly done this before.

"Eggs!"

"Eggs?"

"Yes, there is a farm not far from here. The farmer disappeared, so it's left open, and there are chickens."

"Chickens? You have to be kidding me. We have to catch chickens?"

"No, we grab the eggs."

We walked down the riverbank to the farm not far from the house. It had three pens full of chickens.

"Who feeds the chickens?" I asked John.

"Me!" he answered very quickly.

"Really?"

"Every day at breakfast time."

We walked up to the first pen. There were seven Ameraucana chickens. They all were sitting in their nests. John moved one chicken and found two eggs.

"One for you, and one for me."

"What happens if the chick comes out?"

"These are too tiny to be a chick. There's only yolk in them."

"Yuck!"

We gathered all the eggs and started to head to the Charlie House. We walked back up the riverbank, singing the *Courageous* song.

"I wish my daughter was here! She would be thirty-five today."

"I'm sorry."

"Don't be; I'm glad I have you here with me."

"I'm glad I'm here also."

"I remember one time—"

The sky made a thunder sound, and the sky parted like a curtain. Seven angels appeared holding trumpets. Then a great fireball started hurtling toward earth.

"Run, get in the house! Shield your eyes with newspaper!" John exclaimed to me on the riverbank.

I zoomed to the house and crawled under the table with newspapers on my head. There was thunder loud enough for the whole world to hear. Then the ground began to shake, and everything started rattling. The mice that lived in the holes were holding hands saying their good-byes. Then the whole earth was lit up by lightning. Trees were cracking and tumbling over. Then the angels all got in a line, and the first one sounded the trumpet. It was a great, loud trumpet sound that could make a hole in your ears. I looked out the window and saw hail and fire mixed together coming from the heavens. It hit the ground hard as rocks. There was ice forming all along the house. But the ice on the house was not clear ice; it was red. It all turned red as soon as it hit the ground. The trees were covered in fire and burning to the ground. Everywhere you looked was fire. Fire was where you walked. Fire was on the trees. But the river was calm, as if nothing was happening. The Charlie House had the same bubble around it that God had around me.

"Why is the house not on fire?"

"Because God is protecting us!"

"That's amazing!"

"God can do some amazing things."

"You got that right!"

All of those things continued for seven days. John had some extra eggs, so we scrambled them under the table. We ate under the table, slept under the table, prayed under the table, and talked under the table. All of those seven days our lives were spent under the table. Sounds of thunder and crashing filled the earth. We got very little sleep. I felt like a toddler screaming for the storm to stop. Red covered the earth, but Satan's smile was shining brighter than the stars. Hell seemed to remain on earth for a long time. Seven days might not seem long, but it is if you're stuck under a table.

One night an earthquake was approaching, and the table crashed on the cooler. All drinks and eggs were gone. We were left hungry for two days.

On the eighth day we found everything still. I walked outside, and it was a battlefield. Dead trees on the ground were covered in blood, ice covered the house, and the grass was also covered in blood. It was a nightmare. Animals were dead all around and covered in blood. We grabbed a bucket and collected water from the river while it was still safe to drink.

CHAPTER 17

"Susan, you asleep yet?" John asked me in a whispered tone.

"No, why?"

"Look out the window!" I got up and tiptoed to the window. "Who is it?" I asked John quietly.

"I have no idea! We should go outside and see." We marched outside to a man sitting on a stump. John went right up to him and spoke to him saying, "Hello, may I help you? Are you lost?"

He answered back. "Yeah, I have no idea where I am."

Before the man said anything back, John told him, "You're in Bass River State Forest!"

"You look familiar. Have I seen you somewhere before?" I asked him as I walked up to him.

"I have never met you. At least I don't think so."

"Why don't you just come right in?" John followed behind me.

"Okay." The guy stood up and followed John to the Charlie House.

"Is everything all right?" I asked him. He entered with a puzzled look.

"Yeah, it's just the house looks big on the outside but very small on the inside."

"This is the only thing I have," John said as he slumped down in a chair.

"I'm not complaining, I'm just—"

I interrupted, saying, "Now what is your name?"

"My name?" he asked confused.

"You know, the one your mother calls you by." John looked out the window, as if he was looking for something.

"I don't quite remember!"

"You don't remember your name?"

"No, do you have one?"

"Why, we all do. I'm Susan, and that's John at the window."

"Susan—that is a very, well, that's an interesting name." John came and sat down with us, and I pushed him over to the corner.

"Do you think this guy is kind of weird?" I asked while peeking over my shoulder.

"I don't know. Let him have some rest."

"Are you sure he can sleep with us?"

"My child, why are you so worried? Everything will turn out fine." We sat back down and asked him more questions. All he answered was, "I don't know" or "I don't remember."

I slept inside that night in case anything strange happened. I slept under the table, but it was better than outside. John slept in his own bed, and tall, strange man with no name slept in a corner. But something was stuck in my brain. I had seen that guy before, but I couldn't remember where. That troubled me; I couldn't go to sleep without knowing where I had seen him. I got up and sat near the window thinking of people I had met, and then I suddenly remembered—Charles, Amanda's husband. He had gone off to work for Abram, but I wondered what happened to him. I decided to wait till morning to ask him.

When Charles woke up, I was the first thing he saw.

"Good morning, Char ... I mean, man. Did you sleep well?"

"Not the best sleep I've had."

"Okay, can I ask you a question?"

"Susan, come help me find some eggs," John almost said over me.

"I'll be there in one minute. So, do you remember where you came from?"

"Like, where I was born?"

"No, before we found you. Where were you?"

"I'm sorry, I can't remember," he stuttered.

"Was it on a field or on a farm?" He stood up and walked to the window. He looked up gracefully and turned back to me.

"I'm sorry, I just can't remember. There is a big thing that I do remember." I got up and put my hand on his shoulder.

"What do you remember?"

"I do remember love."

"Love?"

"Yeah, I remember seeing my loved one and kissing her."

"What was her name?" He looked back at the window and leaned forward. His head was on the window. Then he walked outside and looked up at the heavens. I followed right behind him.

"Her name was Amanda, but she's dead."

"You remember?"

"I told you I remember the big things. How could I forget my one true love?"

"But you don't remember your name?"

"Only the big things!" Then he walked back inside.

John came in with the eggs that he had recovered from the storm. "Never mind, I found some!"

There was a second trumpet sound, so we all hid under the table. For about an hour, nothing happened. Everything was normal, so we got out the Bible to see what had just happened. We turned to Revelation 8:8. John read out loud: "Then the second angel sounded. And something like a great mountain burning with fire was thrown into the sea, and a third of the sea became blood. And a third of the living sea creatures died, and a third of the ships were destroyed."

"So that's why we didn't see anything. We don't live near the ocean," I exclaimed, standing up. The man walked over to me.

"You people believe in this junk."

"Of course—why wouldn't we?"

"Because, it's not real! Get that in your heads."

"Why don't you believe in God?"

"I've said He's not rea—"

"What I mean is, why do you think He's not real?"

"He's never done anything for me."

John stood up. "That's what I thought. I was you before everything became crazy, and I thought that for thirty years. I was standing right where you stood now," John told the man.

"But God changed his heart, and now he believes." I told him.

"Okay whatever; I think we need some eggs." He stomped out the door with the egg box walking toward the farm.

I turned to John and told him, "And he only remembers the big things!" He nodded and got a fire going and started boiling the eggs.

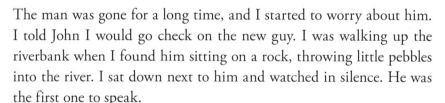

The man was gone for a long time, and I started to worry about him. I told John I would go check on the new guy. I was walking up the riverbank when I found him sitting on a rock, throwing little pebbles into the river. I sat down next to him and watched in silence. He was the first one to speak.

"Why are you here?"

"I was wondering if you were okay. Did you get the eggs, Charles? I, uh, I uh, I mean!"

"Spill!" he screamed at me.

"I know who you are. I lived with you and Amanda. I was the pastor at your wedding, and I ate dinner with you. You went off to go work for Abram. When you came back the house was gone, and now you're here. What happened? Why are you losing your memory? Why is it that you can remember that God is not real but can't remember your name?"

"I can remember other stuff too!"

"Like?"

"My love!"

"Is that all?"

"God is not real!"

"You've told me that!"

"I don't know!" He put his hand over his forehead, got up, and walked back to the Charlie House. I sat for a minute and thought, *How could he have lost his memory?* Then it hit me. In the *Left Behind* movie, the Antichrist brainwashed everyone at the meeting. He must have brainwashed all of his farm workers. He made them forget the unimportant things and made them believe God was not real. What a clump nugget.

CHAPTER 18

John got up bright and early to fetch some water from the river. Charles woke me up to go with him to get the eggs.

"Why do you need me?" I asked him with a sleepy eye.

"I don't know where it is," he told me in a whisper.

"I thought you went out yesterday to get some?"

"I needed an excuse to get out of the house." I got up and went with him to get the eggs.

When we came back, John was getting ready to start the fire when someone knocked on the door. I got up out of my seat and opened the door. No one was there, but there on the burned grass was a bottle. I picked it up, and it had a sticker on it. It said:

Medicine only to be used by Susan.
Use for sickness.
For no one else's use.

"What is it?" John asked me.

"Something that the mailman dropped off for me. At least I think it's by the mailman."

"What did he drop off?"

"Medicine … to be used only by me."

'dd!"

it
ep

———————⌢———————

getting ready for bed, the third trumpet sounded. We
gain hid under the table. We saw a burning light that
ray. A great big ball of fire was shooting across the sky
me down like a burning torch. A grand fire spread
ne inch at a time. But the Charlie House never got
utterly surprise came upon the rivers and the lakes.
ucket of water and took a sip.

bitter!" John screamed with his tongue out.

arles dunked his cup in the bucket and took a sip.

Susan, you try!" I dunked my cup in the bucket

so. He   bitter."

goes away, I'll get some more water from the lake."
bitter?" Charles asked John.

le until we find water. I don't know." When the fire
walked out the door and poured out the water. Then
ket. He came in hacking and hacking.

ay?" I asked him as he sat down in his chair.

My throat hurts, and my …" He hacked again. "And
when I cough."

have a cold?" I guessed when I eyed the bottle of

" He put his hand over his forehead. "It's
mometer. He put it in his mouth

pen mouth.

ran over to look at it. It was 104.5.

nis?"

"I don't know. I just feel so sleepy," he said with a yawn.

"You get some rest!" I eyed the medicine again and wondered if would hurt for him to use it. I nudged Charles, but he was fast asle also.

John took about a three-hour nap and woke up with swollen eyes.

"John, you look horrible."

"My child, this is part of God's plan."

"How come you're not worried?"

"I am worried; I just don't want to show it."

"Want to use the medicine I got?"

"That's only supposed to be used by you."

"So, it says use for sickness. Why can't you use it?"

"Susan, please don't!"

"I'll think about it." Charles woke up with swollen eyes a was hacking left and right.

"Are you okay?" John asked Charles in a weak voice.

"No! I don't feel so well! I can't feel my throat."

"It's gotten to you. It must be contagious!"

"Susan, do something!" Charles screamed as loud as his vo let him. I looked again at the bottle. I read the symptoms the should be used for, all of which John and Charles had. W choice did I have? They needed help, and I had the cure. I g the directions that said to take one tablet and no more, but three tablets in the box. Maybe one was for John, one was fo and one was for me if I got sick. I opened the lid and too tablets and handed them out.

"I thought it can only be used for you," Charles said, tak from my hand.

"What am I supposed to do? Sit here and see you ge I have a cure under my nose?"

"My child, you have done wrong," John proclaimed to me in a weak voice.

"Then don't take it!"

"I'm sorry, I have to!" He opened his mouth and shoved it in. Charles followed right behind him. I sat down and started rubbing my throat.

"My throat—I can't feel it!"

"Oh no, it's already gotten to you." Charles turned to me. He asked me, "You feel hot?"

I put my hand to my forehead and nodded my head. I took the last tablet out of the bottle and shoved it in my mouth. All three of us were lying on the floor, sick as dogs. John looked awful, Charles looked a little better than John, and I don't know what I looked like. I didn't even want to know.

We huddled in the covers, and it took Charles and me a very long time to get to sleep. John slept like a baby. We hacked all night, waking each other up. Charles hogged the covers. He would pull them all to his side and leave us freezing in the open air. John got up a couple of times feeling nauseated. He said he only threw up once during the night. He started complaining to the wall about how his stomach hurt. Charles only got up once, and he had to use the toilet. I did as well. John was the one who had it bad. I knew he couldn't last long with his old body. This would be too hard on his body if he kept feeling this way for long.

CHAPTER 19

"I don't think this medicine is working," Charles told me. He looked even worse than yesterday. His throat was swollen and purple. John was the same way. I felt queasy and weak. We all lay on the floor the whole day. Poor John—he was trying to make himself look strong. Charles had an amazed look on his face, so I crawled over to him.

"You okay?" I asked him.

"I remember you! You're Susan, the one who I lived with. I ate dinner with you, and you were the pastor at our wedding."

"I told you that the other day."

"I know, but I remember you telling me that. I was born in New York, I went to Atlantic City High School, I graduated in '88, and I married Amanda a couple weeks ago."

"He's back! How did you get your memory back?"

"Amanda!"

"Amanda? She's not here!"

"I found Amanda's Bible and read the note, and it had been on my mind. I didn't think God was real, but now I'm not so sure." John eased up out of his chair.

"Oh, it's happening! Susan, you do it."

"Do what? What's happening?"

70

"Something I have been waiting for."

"My memory?"

"No, my child, your faith!" John said in a weak voice.

"My faith? What about my faith?"

"Susan! Why don't you do it?" I picked up my Bible and turned to John 19. I sat down right beside him and began to read.

> So then Pilate took Jesus and scourged Him. And the soldiers twisted a crown of thorns and put it on His head, and they put on Him a purple robe. Then they said, "Hail, King of the Jews!" And they struck Him with their hands. Pilate then went out again, and said to them, "Behold I am bringing Him out to you, that you may know that I find no fault in Him." Then Jesus came out wearing the crown of thorns and the purple robe. And Pilate said to them, "Behold the Man!" Therefore, when the chief priests and officers saw Him, they cried out, saying, "Crucify Him, crucify Him!" Pilate said to them, "You take Him, crucify Him, for I find no fault in Him." Then the Jews answered him, "We have a law and according to our law He ought to die, because He made himself the Son of God." Therefore, when Pilate heard that saying, he was the more afraid, and went again into the Praetorium, and said to Jesus, "Where are You from?" But Jesus gave him no answer. Then Pilate said to him, "Are You not speaking to me? Do You not know that I have power to crucify You, and power to release you?" Jesus answered, "You could have no power at all against Me unless it had been given you from above. Therefore the one who delivered Me to you has the greater sin."

"Okay, that's enough, I understand!" Charles told me before I could continue reading.

"You understand why Jesus died on the cross?"

"No, I understand that Jesus was a fake. All the people were crying out, 'Crucify him.' I will do the same!"

That just broke my heart. My heart became weak and felt like it could not beat. It was shattered and torn apart. John put his hand on my hand and told me to keep on trying.

"Don't ever give up, my child!"

I flipped to the empty tomb part of John. "Do you want some good news, Charles?"

"Sure, why not? Is it going to be from that fake Bible?"

"It sure is, and you better get yourself comfy because you are going to listen. I began to read from the Good Book.

> Now the first day of the week Mary Magdalene went to the tomb early, while it was still dark, and saw that the stone had been taken away from the tomb. Then she ran and came to Simon Peter, and to the other disciple, whom Jesus loved, and said to them, "They have taken away the Lord out of the tomb, and we do not know where they have laid Him." Peter therefore went out, and the other disciple, and were going to the tomb. So they both ran together, and the other disciple outran peter and came to the tomb first. And he, stooping down and looking in, saw the linen cloths lying there; yet he did not go in. Then Simon Peter came, following him, and went into the tomb; and he saw the linen cloths lying there, and the handkerchief that had been around his head, not lying with the linen cloths, but folded together in a place by itself. Then the other disciple, who came to the tomb first, went in also; and he saw and believed. For as yet they did not know the Scripture, that he must rise again from the dead. Then the disciples went away again to their own homes. But Mary stood outside by the tomb weeping, and as she wept she stooped down and looked into the tomb. And she saw two angels in while sitting, one at the

head and the other at the feet, where the body of Jesus had lain. Then they said to her. "Woman, why are you weeping?" She said to them, "Because they have taken away my Lord, and I do not know where they have laid him." Now when she had said this, she turned around and saw Jesus standing there, and did not know that it was Jesus. Jesus said to her, "Woman, why are you weeping? Whom are you seeking?" She supposing Him to be the gardener, said to Him, "Sir if you have carried Him away, tell me where you have laid Him, and I will take Him away." Jesus said to her, "Mary!" She turned and said to Him, "Rabboni!" Jesus said to her, "Do not cling to Me, for I have not yet ascended to My father; but go to My brethren and say to them, "I am ascending to my father and your father, and to my God and your God." Mary Magdalene came and told the disciples that she had seen the Lord, and that He had spoken these things to her.

"Okay, that still doesn't prove He is real. Someone could have made that up. If God didn't write the Bible, then who did?"

"Eye-witnesses!"

"So, ordinary people?"

"Every book is like that."

"Then why is this one special?"

"God told men what to write; they're His words." John looked at Charles and asked him.

"Who made you the way you are? Who made this earth that you live on? Who made wonderful creatures that you see?"

"Science!"

"Can science explain why whales sing?"

"Yes!"

"Can identify what they're singing?"

"No!"

"See, science can't explain all of life's mysteries."

"Okay, but there is no proof that humans can come back to life."

"Oh, my child, yes there is—the Bible!" John said.

Charles's faced turned red, and he ended the conversation with, "The Bible is a stupid book that some idiots wrote just to make things a little interesting."

John closed his eyes and fell asleep. But before he did so, he told me, "My child, people will disappoint you in life, but never forget this: God has a big plan for what He can do with just a simple conversation. You may have planted a seed that may need some watering over the days, but soon it will sprout and make you joyful. I will not see it, but I will see you in heaven. Never give up, my child; never give up!" He closed his eyes with the biggest smile on his face, and his soul went up into the sky.

I whispered back, "I will not give up. I promise!"

CHAPTER 20

C harles checked John's heart rate and found that his heart was no longer beating. I cried in the corner for hours, praying he could come back to life. John was a good man with a kind heart and a kind soul. I wrote down what he told me before he passed away and hid it under my clothes. Charles had red eyes but never cried. I didn't understand why he didn't cry. John was a wonderful person; I guess Charles never knew that because he was not a follower of Jesus.

I went through all his clothes and junk that he had crammed in the drawer of his dresser. I found pictures of his family. One was taken at Niagara Falls; his beautiful blond wife was in the middle, with three children around her. The one on the right looked like a thirteen-year-old, the one on the left looked like an eight-year-old, and the last one in front of their mom was about five. The thirteen-year-old had brown hair like her dad with glasses, the eight-year-old had brown hair as well, and the five-year-old had blond hair with a bow on the side. John stood beside his wife with his arm around her. He had a good-looking family, but such a sad story. I took out the picture and placed it in John's arms and whispered in his cold, dead ear, "I know you're dancing in heaven with your beautiful family."

Charles, on the other hand, was sneezing and coughing every second. He started looking worse.

"Charles, are you doing okay?" I asked him, walking over to where he was laying.

"Does it look like I'm okay? I have never felt more miserable in my life. First I lose my wife, house, memory, and friend, and now maybe my life."

"You don't know that!"

"I have the same thing that John had, and look what happened to him."

"His body could not keep him on his feet, so he had to pass on."

"I think I'm ready to pass on!" he told me in a fake death moment.

"Oh, stop that, no you're not. You will be just okay."

"How do you know?"

"I don't know! Only God knows!"

"Oh, I don't want to hear another word." He put his hands over his ears, and we spoke no more.

I took a little walk outside so I could get away from the body. I talked to God, "Lord, I am here to worship and follow You. Give me the words to say, obedience, patience, and strength. I know this is all coming from You, Lord. Let him live long enough for me to talk to him. He needs You more than he will ever know. Let him believe in Your name and Your name only. Thank You, Lord, for leading me here. Amen!" At that same moment the fourth trumpet sounded, and I ran as fast as my legs would carry me to the Charlie House. I plummeted through the front door.

"Hurry, get under the table!" I told Charles as I was racing to the table.

"Why do we need to get under the table?"

"The fourth trumpet sounded, and I don't know what crazy thing is going to happen."

"There is no way I'm hiding under a table."

"Okay!" He lay down on the floor. "Are you doing okay?"

"I think you can answer that!" he said, followed by a sneeze. Then there was a loud strike. There was fire from heaven, then the moon got struck by fire, and following it was the stars. The whole earth went black in an instant.

"Got any room under the table?" Charles asked me, trying to stand up.

"Yes, come on!"

He walked slowly over to the table and crouched down. "What just happened?"

"From what I read, a third of the daytime will be dark."

"What book did you find that out of?"

"The Bible!" I grabbed my Bible and turned to Revelation. "See, the fourth trumpet, then the fourth angel sounded; and a third of the sun was struck, a third of the moon, and a third of the stars, so that a third of them were darkened. A third of the day did not shine, and likewise the night. And I looked, and I heard an angel flying through the midst of heaven, saying with a loud voice, 'woe, woe, woe to the inhabitants of the earth, because of the remaining blasts of the trumpet of the three angels who are about to sound!' See, everything that the Bible predicted is coming true."

"Maybe it's just a coincidence."

"Really? Are you just saying that?"

"Yes, maybe part of the Bible is telling the truth."

"Maybe part of the dictionary is telling the truth."

"Stop using my own words against me."

"Why do you hate the Bible that much?"

"I don't; it's just not real!"

"Why do you think the Bible is not real?"

"Really? Look at it—people coming back to life, healing of a blind man, healing of a man with leprosy, people walking on water, and demon-possessed men."

"Nothing is impossible with God. He can do all things, if you believe He can."

"Okay, enough of this chatter. Let's get back to reality."

"No, this is reality, and the Bible is true."

"Think what you want to think. Have you ever wondered if you're wrong?"

"What do you mean?"

"Well, Muslims think that they're right. Have you thought that maybe you're wrong?"

"Of course I have!" I said with a smile.

"That was not the response I thought you were going to give."

"We all have our doubts. Do you have doubts about things?"

"On some things!"

"See, we all doubt things. That's what makes us human."

"What are you trying to say?"

"I'm saying that I have doubted God, but His grace always breaks through."

"Whatever!" He tried standing up but fell back on his knees.

"Where are you trying to go?"

"The window, to see what the outside world looks like." I helped him up and followed him to the window. The earth was black. "So, this is what I'm going to live with the rest of my life?"

"A dark and falling world, yes."

He fell back into his chair and fell asleep. I, on the other hand, stood up, watching the dark and empty world fall on top of the unbelievers.

CHAPTER 21

After Charles awoke from his nap, we grabbed some flashlights and buried John in the dark. We buried him right next to his favorite chicken coop. His family picture was still in his hands. I cried my way back to the Charlie House, while Charles caught my tears. He didn't even shed a single tear.

When we got back, Charles flopped down on his chair and called me over to his seat. "Can we talk?"

"Of course. You can talk to me about anything, like maybe your faith."

"No, I was just wondering if you can tell me about your family."

"My family?"

"Yeah, what was your family like?"

"Why do you want to know?"

"You're such a nice young lady, and I was wondering where you got that from."

"Okay, well, I loved my father more than my mother. He was kind to me and did not yell at my mother. My mother loved to raise her voice at my father. She worked at a bank as a teller, and my father was a shoe salesman."

"Neat! Did you get free shoes?"

"No, but we did get a discount. Mom was a kind woman who always liked to get in your face and boss you around."

"Parents don't boss their kids around; they just tell them what to do."

"That's the meaning of bossing people around!"

"No, they tell you what is good for you."

"Anyway, my mother loved to watch her crime shows, like *Law and Order*. My father, on the other hand, loved spending time with me. He didn't care if Jane White got killed. He would go up to my room to see if I was doing okay when Mother would scream at the TV. I would say I'm a lot like my father. But my mother loved God more than my father. She loved going to church. One year she never missed a Sunday. She went when she was sick, and when she was fifteen days past her due date—"

"You were born late? Well that explains a lot."

"No, my brother was."

"Your brother?"

"Yeah. I don't like talking about him."

"Did he disappear?"

"No, he died at birth." I grabbed one of his tissues and blew my nose.

"I'm sorry. I didn't know."

"It's not your fault. Anyway, I should get some rest. I don't know if it's even nighttime."

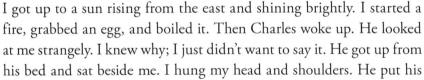

I got up to a sun rising from the east and shining brightly. I started a fire, grabbed an egg, and boiled it. Then Charles woke up. He looked at me strangely. I knew why; I just didn't want to say it. He got up from his bed and sat beside me. I hung my head and shoulders. He put his hand on my shoulder.

"Why are you so upset?" he asked me in a sick voice.

"I don't want to say."

"It will make you feel better if you get it off of your chest."

"No, it will make it worse."

"Sure?"

"Yes!"

"Come on, whatever it is, you can get through it."

"Fine, since you really want to know." I slowly raised my volume. "Today is my birthday. My dad isn't here, and all my friends are dead."

"If you want a present, I can get you one."

"That's not it. My parents aren't here to hug me or tell me happy birthday."

"My parents weren't here to hug me on my birthday. They're gone as well."

"Well, at your age, that's normal. I'm turning sixteen! That's a big deal."

"What about kids who don't have parents?"

"Well, I had parents!"

"So did those kids, and their parents just left them."

"I guess you're right!"

"You guess?"

"Okay, you're right." I put my egg on my plate and gobbled it down. Charles made his and ate little pieces at a time.

"Are you feeling better?" I asked Charles as he ate slowly.

"No, I don't feel any better. I don't think that medicine worked."

"Next time I won't let you take medicine from the mailman."

"Yes, please don't. How come you're not sick?"

"Well, if you count a stuffy nose and coughing, I am."

"That is the first phase."

"Don't worry about me. Let me just worry about you."

"Tell me why you are so kind."

"I'm a follower of Jesus. He is in my heart; He changed me. I didn't get it from my parents. I got it from God."

"Ha, ha, very funny, now tell me the real reason." He laughed hysterically.

"I'm not joking. God changed me. Why can't you understand that? Why are you so against it?"

"Because, it's ridiculous!"

"Why do you think it's ridiculous?"

"It's, it's—I don't know, just so hard to believe."

"Why is it hard to believe?"

"Everyone says it's not real."

"Not everyone! Who is everyone?"

"My wife!"

"Your wife?"

"She was the love of my life, and I liked what she liked, hated what she hated. One of the things was God. So I've never believed in God."

"She's a Christian now!"

"So? She's dead. I don't need to impress her anymore."

"Can't you believe what you want to believe?"

"Yes, I just wanted to impress Amanda. She made a good statement about God. There is nothing that can change me."

"I wouldn't bet on that."

"Like you can change my mind?"

"Maybe I can't, but God can."

"You make me so mad! *Stop talking about God!*" He screamed as loud as he could and scrambled to get outside.

"Happy birthday to me!"

I got up and wrote a letter to Dad, telling him how much I missed him. I folded it, put it in an envelope, addressed it to heaven, and placed it in the mailbox. Then I came in and blew my nose and started crying my eyes out. When I heard the door open, I looked up and saw Dad standing there. He was wearing his, "I'm a father of an angel" shirt and his blue jeans. I threw my tissue away and put a smile on my face. I got up and then walked toward him.

"Daddy, I miss you!"

He answered, "I know, but I can't stay, I just wanted to say I love you and happy birthday." As I got my arms ready to hug him, he disappeared, and that's when I knew I had imagined him. He wasn't there to tell me happy birthday. He wasn't there to tell me he loved me, and he wasn't there to hug me. I picked up that tissue and wiped every tear that came down my sixteen-year-old face.

CHAPTER 22

I found Charles passed out by the river. He had fallen and hit his head on a rock. His head and face were bleeding. I dragged him to the house and sat him down on the couch. I beat his chest for ten minutes while talking to him.

"Charles, Charles, please wake up! Come on, wake up, please, Charles!" I started crying when after the fiftieth beat I gave up. I bowed my head and prayed to God that Charles would wake up. When I lifted my head, Charles got up and rubbed his head.

"What happened?"

"You fell and hit your head on a rock. Are you okay?"

"I guess. What is this coming out of my head?"

"I'll get you a bandage." I walked over to John's medicine box and took out a bandage. I put it on Charles's wound that was on his head and wrapped it with the bandage.

"I remember being mad at you. I walked outside, came upon the river, tripped over a rock, and then I was out. How did you wake me up?"

"I didn't wake you up!"

"Who woke me up then?" Charles asked me in a panicky voice.

"Why don't you try to guess?"

"Oh, please don't tell me you think God did it."

"God did do it!"

"Oh, please!"

"I prayed, and when I lifted my head, you woke up. Please don't tell me something hurtful because, one, it's my birthday, two, I don't need that right now, and three, well I don't need a third one."

"Fine, I won't say anything, but you know my opinion."

I heard the fifth trumpet sound. Charles jumped up.

"Was that a trumpet?"

"Get under the table!"

"No, I want to see what's happening."

"You want to see what's happening?" I picked up my Bible and began to read about the fifth trumpet.

> Then the fifth angel sounded, and I saw a star fallen from heaven to the Earth. To him was given the key to the bottomless pit. And he opened the bottomless pit and smoke arose out of the pit like the smoke of a great furnace. So the sun and the air were darkened because of the smoke of the pit. Then out of the smoke locusts came upon the earth. And to them was given power, as the scorpions of the earth have power. They were commanded not to harm the grass of the earth, or any green thing, or any tree, but only those men who do not have the seal of God on their foreheads. And they were not given authority to kill them, but to torment them for five months. Their torment was like the torment of a scorpion when it strikes a man. In those days men will seek death and will not find it, they will desire to die, and death will flee from them. The shape of the locust was like horses prepared for battle. On their heads were crowns of something like gold, and their

faces were like the faces of men. They had hair like women's hair, and their teeth were like the lions teeth. And they had breastplates like breastplates of iron, and the sound of their wings was like the sound of chariots with many horses running into battle. They had tails like scorpions and there were stings in their tail. Their power was to hurt men five months. And they had as king over them the angel of the bottomless pit, whose name in Hebrew is Abaddon, but in Greek he has the name Apollyon. One woe is past. Behold, still two more woes are coming after these things.

"Wow! I would become a Christian if I were you."

"Nah, I'll see if that really happens."

"You know that it will really happen. Why don't you just believe?"

"Does it bother you that bad that I'm not a Christian?"

"Yes, because I don't want you to go to Hell." The earth suddenly became bright as the sun. I rushed over to the window and saw the earth almost blowing up. It was too bright for us to look out. We got back under the table when the planet jumped with fear. Then it darkened quickly, and a large key fell from the heavens and crashed into the ground. The ground shook like a paint mixer machine as the key blasted the ground. Then smoke arose from the ground like a bonfire. Then in the distance I heard chariots racing into battle.

"Uh-oh, do you hear that?"

"Yes, it sounds like horses!"

"Did you hear anything I read?"

"Is it scorpions?"

"No, it's locusts, and they're coming for you."

"Right, the locusts that will torment me for five months," he said to me sarcastically. Then the chariots started getting louder and louder until they reached the front door. They all started swarming in like bats coming into their cave. They all headed toward Charles. They looked exactly like what John described: crowns on their heads, faces like men's faces, breastplates made of iron, and long hair. They were ready for battle. Charles screamed like a little girl.

"Susan, help me. I need a tissue!" Charles screamed at me.

"Do you need it for your nose or your heart?"

"My nose—what else would I use it for?"

"Maybe to patch up what's been missing in your heart?" He had locusts all over him. I could barely see his face.

"Oh, let me just kill myself." He stumbled around the room, found a gun, and pointed it toward himself.

"No, you'll just make things worse. Please don't pull that trigger."

"I cannot let these bugs torment me for five months. Plus, I'm sick."

"You can make them stop by becoming a Christian." He pulled the trigger.

Kaboom! But nothing happened. He pulled it again.

Kaboom! He checked the bullets.

"There are still a ton in there."

"I told you, shooting yourself will not solve the problem."

"What's the way to get the locusts off?"

"I told you, become a Christian."

"How do I do that?" The locusts started slowly moving away.

"You pray to God and ask Him into your heart. You believe that Jesus died on the cross and rose from the dead, and He did it for us. If you believe in that and tell Him that you believe, He will enter your heart."

"If God did all this, then Jesus' death must be true. I have never felt this great before. I feel an overwhelming peace and happiness."

"If you ask Him to come into your heart, then you will have peace for the rest of eternity." He bowed his head and prayed by himself; one by one the locusts started flying off of him and right out the door. He had the seal of God on his forehead. No one could tell him differently.

CHAPTER 23

"Charles, are you okay?" I sat beside him on the bed.

"No, I think my time is coming up. I feel horrible."

"Don't worry. I don't feel so well either."

"No, I mean—"

"I know what you mean. It's going to be okay."

"I don't know!" Charles was talking in a weak voice. He closed his eyes and opened them really quickly.

"What was that for?"

"To make sure I'm alive." He said in a lower whisper.

"What? Speak up."

"To make sure I'm alive."

"To make sure you're alive?" He nodded. I felt woozy, and I fell to the ground.

"Susan, what happened to you?" He tried to scream, but I barely heard it.

Then I fell asleep. I could not find enough words to say how I was feeling. Let me just say I felt queasy.

I got off of the floor and found Charles still asleep on the bed. I went over to check on him, and his heart was not beating. He was cold, and that's when I realized he had died in his sleep. I wept on his body and was thankful he had gone to heaven. Out of the corner of my eye, I saw a horse in the window. I ran outside and saw horses flying in the sky. One horse had a head of a lion, and out came fire. The men who sat on the horses had breastplates that were fiery red. One horse came down to me and stared at me. I was afraid of what he was going to do to me. Then he looked at a scroll and left. I raced to the Bible and read out loud.

> Then the sixth angel sounded: and I heard a voice from the four horns of the golden altar which is before God, saying to the sixth angel who had the trumpet, "Release the four angels who are bound at the great river Euphrates." So the four angels, who had been prepared for the hour and day and month and year, were released to kill a third of mankind. Now the number of the army of the horsemen was two hundred million; I heard the number of them. And thus I saw the horses in the vision: those who sat on them had breastplate of fiery red, hyacinth blue, and sulfur yellow; and the heads of the horses were like the heads of lions; and out of their mouths came fire, smoke, and brimstone. By those three plagues a third of mankind was killed by the fire, smoke, and the brimstone which came out of their mouths. For their power is in their mouth and in their tails; for their tails are like serpents, having heads; and with them they do no harm. But the rest of mankind who were not killed by these plagues, did not repent of the works of their hands, that they should not worship demands, and idols of gold, silver, brass, stone, and wood, which can neither see nor hear nor walk. And they did not repent of their sorcerers or their sexual immorality or their thefts.

I looked up at Charles and sat beside him on the bed. I said to him almost in a whisper, "I am going to miss you, but I'm happy that you're in a better place. I have never said this to any of my household guests, but you were my favorite. I knew that deep down you still believed in Jesus. There was just something that made you not believe."

I wept for days over the loss of Charles West. What was I going to do? Where would God send me now? I felt woozy all of the sudden, like I did before. I stumbled to the couch and fell on it. My head started pounding and throbbing. My stomach was not doing so great either. I put my hand over my head, and it almost burned my hand. I knew I had a fever of 103 something. I was getting weaker and weaker until my eyes started shutting down. I was on the edge of dying, but I knew I wasn't going to die. It was God speaking to me through my sleep. I was asleep, but I wasn't asleep.

I had a vision of a house with a Catholic family living in it. There was the father, Richard, the twenty-year-old son, Ralph, the mother, Virginia, the eighteen-year-old daughter, Gloria, and their turtle, RG. Richard was an insurance agent, Virginia was an accountant, and Ralph worked at Sears. Gloria wanted to never work a day in her life. She got paid for looking pretty at Macys. This family had some issues. They loved Jesus, but they were not Christians. They thought they were saved because they had been baptized. The family lived in Ventnor City, right near Atlantic City. They were having dinner when I saw them in my vision. They looked like a happy family, but they needed Christ.

I woke up, took Charles outside, and buried him near the stump where I found him.

Five months later …

I said a prayer, packed my things, and was on my way (as best as I could) to Ventnor City. I took another nap on a park bench. A couple of people looked at me as strangely, as if I were a polar bear. They screamed and ran off, and I just sat there wondering what they were screaming at. Finally I looked at my reflection in some broken glass and saw myself—broken down and worn out. I had never seen someone who looked more awful. I looked worse than homeless people. I traveled for ten days looking for the house with four broken people living in it. The whole town looked like what I had seen in my vision.

On the tenth day I came upon a confused house. The house had red brick on all four sides, with five bedrooms, and three baths. They had a southern porch that wrapped around the house, which was odd in New Jersey. I went up to the front door and rang the doorbell. A young beautiful girl answered.

"Ah-ah-ah!" she screamed, and then she closed the door in my face. I looked down at the ground when the door opened again. This time a tall, brown-haired lady answered

"I am so sorry. My daughter screams when she sees hideous things. So may I help you?"

"Yes, I was wondering if you could give me a place to stay."

"I'm sorry, we don't take in strangers. Try our neighbors. Have a nice day." She almost closed the door.

"Wait. I was sent here by God. Can you spare me your extra bedroom?"

"Sent here by God, you say?"

"Yes, in a vision!"

"Well, the church always wants us to help out people."

"Does that mean I can stay?"

"Sure, come on in!"

CHAPTER 24

She walked me upstairs to the extra bedroom. She told me where the bathroom was because she said I needed to take a shower. I didn't blame her; I did stink.

"Lunch will be prepared shortly." She told me.

"Thank you so much for giving me a place to stay."

"No problem!" She left the room, and I unpacked my things and fell down on the bed.

About twenty minutes into my nap, the seventh trumpet sounded. I got myself up and wobbled downstairs. I heard Gloria talking to her mother, "Mom, why can't I go out into the world and get my own place?"

"Gloria, right now is not the right time."

"Why not?"

"Gloria, you should never ask your mother, 'Why not?'" I slowly walked into the kitchen.

"Is everybody doing okay?" I asked them.

"No, Mom will not let me go out on my own. I'm eighteen, which means I can leave the house," she said on the way out of the kitchen. I looked out the window and saw hail as big as a baseball.

"Oh my weather, that is some big hail." Virginia screamed. I heard footsteps running down the stairs like a stampede.

"Mom, did you see what's outside?" someone screamed from halfway down the stairs. I looked over my shoulder and saw a big, handsome young man. He had blond hair, blue eyes, and a dreamy face.

"Yes, they're huge. I have never seen anything like it before." He came by me, and I was flattered.

"Who is this?" He asked.

"This is … What is your name?" Virginia asked me.

"Susan, Susan Douglas. Nice to meet you, Ralph." I stuck out my hand for him to shake it.

"Susan, how do you know my name?" He didn't return the favor. I put my hand back in its usual place.

"I had a vision about you."

"That's really flattering, but I have a girlfriend."

"No, I mean, God sent me here. He told me about all of you. You have an eighteen-year-old sister, Gloria, a father named Richard, a mother named Virginia, and a turtle named RG." He just stared at me with a blank face. I looked back at the window. Then a great thunder roared from the west.

"Looks like we're going to have a storm tonight. What do you think?" When Virginia turned around to look at me, I was already heading out the kitchen door. "Hon, are you doing okay?"

"Yeah, I'm just a little sick."

"A little? You need some medicine."

"I've got medicine, but thank you."

"It's not working!"

"I'll be fine; you don't have to worry about me." I wobbled back up the stairs when the house lit up like a light bulb from lightning.

"It's getting closer!" Virginia screamed so the house could hear her.

I went up to the bathroom and took a shower. It poured and poured, with winds blowing across the sky. Thunder crashed, baseballs fell from the sky, and lightning alternated with the thunder. It was a mess outside.

I went downstairs for lunch, and I sat by Ralph. Richard started the conversation.

"So, Susan, how old are you?"

"I turned sixteen a few months ago."

"Happy late birthday, then!" Virginia said to me.

"Thank you. So tell me about yourself."

Gloria spoke first. "I own one hundred fifty-six pairs of high-heeled shoes, one hundred twenty-three flats, one hundred seventy-eight sandals, one hundred forty-three boots, one hundred eight dresses, one hundred twenty-nine pants, one hundred fifty-six shirts, and seven skirts. I don't like skirts, but I do love other clothes."

"Wow, okay. What about you, Dream Face—I mean Ralph?"

"I work at Sears. Girls think I'm dreamy, but I've got my own gal to think about. Athena is the love of my life. We've been together since ninth grade. She is the peanut to my butter, the pop to my corn, and the best to my friend."

"I got it! Virginia, what about you?"

"I love to do projects, like with pallet wood, I do a lot of DIYs. I love to sew and make clothes. I like the DIY Network and Home and Garden Channel. I spend most of my time doing projects, as you can see."

"Cool, Richard, tell me about you."

"In my spare time I like to golf. Golfing was my passion when I was a teenager. I wanted to be a professional golfer. But when I had kids, my dream was to be the best father to my kids. Now, Susan, tell us about you."

"I'm Baptist, and I live for Jesus. That pretty much sums me up."

"Well, we're Catholic, and we also love Jesus," Richard explained to me. Virginia got up to put her plate in the sink, and Gloria followed behind her.

She went back to the table and told us, "I have to go color code my many clothes."

Ralph got up as well and said, "Today is Tuesday, workout day, so I'm off."

"Today is Thursday!" Virginia screamed to Ralph, who was already out the door.

"He doesn't like hanging out with his family."

"One day he'll wish that he had," I whispered to myself.

"Did you say something?" Richard asked me.

"Yeah, what do you believe in?"

"What do I believe in? I don't follow you."

"What do you think about the rapture?"

"Oh, is that when Jesus takes up Christians to heaven?"

"Yes, that's what it is!"

"I believe in it. Why do you want to know?"

"Because, I have something to tell you. Please, don't say anything until I am done. I know I am right."

Virginia came and sat down.   "What do you have to tell us?"

"You've missed the boat ..." Thunder boomed and lightning answered.

"What are you tal—"

"I said let me finish. The rapture has already happened. The trumpets are part of the tribulation. You have been left behind."

"No! That's not possible."

"Are you a Christian?"

"Yes, of course we are!"

"Then why are you left behind?" It took a while for her to answer.

"I don't know!"

"Why do you think you're Christians?"

"Because we were baptized."

"That doesn't mean you are Christians."

"Yes, it does!" Virginia got up and left the room.

"I have to agree with her." Richard got up and left the room also. When I put my hands to my head, the storm stopped. Everything was calm!

CHAPTER 25

I was in my room reading the Bible when Gloria came in.

"What did you do to my mom?"

"What do you mean?" I closed my Bible and set it down on the bedside table.

"She's in her room calling our priest and asking him stupid questions that she knows the answer to."

"What were the questions?"

"What do you do to become a Christian? Do you think I'm a Christian? Has the rapture happened yet? Will I go to heaven when I die?"

"I talked to her at lunch, and she didn't agree with me."

"What did you say?"

"I asked her if she was a Christian and told her that the rapture has already happened."

"If the rapture has already happened, then why are you still here?"

"I asked God to stay."

"That is the most ridiculous thing I have ever heard."

"I'm just trying to stop people from going to Hell."

"We're not going to Hell!" I picked up my Bible and turned to Luke 13:24

"Listen to this:

> 'Make every effort to enter through the narrow door, because many, I tell you, will try to enter and will not be able to. Once the owner of the house gets up to close the door, you will stand outside knocking and pleading, 'sir open the door for us.' But he will answer, 'I don't know you or where you came from.' Then you will say, 'we ate and drank with you, and you taught in our streets.' But he will reply, 'I don't know you or where you come from. Away from me, all you evildoers!' There will be weeping there, and gnashing of teeth, when you see Abraham, Isaac and Jacob and all the prophets in the kingdom of God, but you yourselves thrown out. People will come from the east and west and north and south, and will take their places at the feast in the kingdom of God. Indeed there are those who are last who will be first, and first who will be last.'"

"What does that even mean?"

"Let's see what the commentary says. 'Finding salvation requires more concentrated effort than most people are willing to put forth. Obviously, we cannot save ourselves—there is no way we can work ourselves into God's favor. The effort we must put out to enter through the narrow door is earnestly desiring to know Jesus and diligently striving to follow Him whatever the cost. We dare not put off making this decision because the door will not stay open forever.' Did that help?"

She walked out of the room with a new perspective.

I was not invited for dinner, so they sent food to my room.

"Sorry, my mom didn't want to see you at dinner, so here's the leftovers," Gloria said as she came into my room.

"Thanks for thinking about me."

"Can I ask you a question?"

"Fire away!"

She sat down on my bed. "What do you have to do to get saved?"

"You have to repent of your sins and ask God into your heart. Then you get baptized. Just because you're baptized doesn't mean that you're saved. You have to pray to God and invite Him into your life."

"So that's what Baptists do, you say?"

"Yes!"

"Okay, thank you!" She got up and walked back to her room.

I sat down on my bed and chomped down on my food. They only gave me a little bean soup with a slice of bread and no drink. But at least it was better than eggs.

I got ready for bed when I heard Gloria and Virginia fighting. I snooped in the hallway until I reached where I could understand them.

"You did what?" Virginia raised her voice at Gloria.

"Mom, you don't understand. I need something more."

"If the church ever found out about this, I would do far more badly than I have ever done to you."

"The church? I wonder what she did at church," I whispered.

"I thought you would be happy for me, but I was wrong."

"Why would I be happy?"

"You always say try new things; this is the one place where I understand things."

"That's against the Catholic rules."

"Well, I don't have to worry about that anymore, because I'm not Catholic. And I never will be!"

She stomped out of her mother's room, and I zoomed into mine, saying a thank-you prayer to God. Gloria understood what I had told her.

I said my night prayers and went to bed, feeling good about what I had accomplished. One down, three to go, and Virginia was not going to be easy. She was very loyal to the Catholic Church and would never want to leave it. It would have to be a miracle from God to change her mind.

CHAPTER 26

I got ready for the day and walked downstairs. The family was already eating breakfast.

"Good morning, everyone. How was your night?" Everyone looked up except for Virginia.

"Good morning, Susan. I slept well—did you?" Gloria answered as she stood up.

"My night was restful." She showed me over to the living room.

"I'm sorry—my mom doesn't want to look at you." She handed me the remote. "Here, you can find something on TV."

"Thank you!" I sat down on the couch and flipped through the channels. Nothing really good was on, so I flipped to the news. I opened my ears to begin to listen to the news when I overheard the family talking.

"Gloria, explain to your father what you did yesterday," Virginia started out.

"What did I do yesterday?"

"Okay, I will tell your father; she quit the Catholic Church." There was silence for a little while. "Well, Richard, what are we going to do?"

"Gloria, you know how she feels about the Catholic Church. What made you decide to leave?"

"Susan helped me realize that I need Jesus more than the Catholic Church told me."

"Okay, maybe we can switch to another Catholic Church."

"No, I'm switching to Baptist. Susan says—" Virginia stopped her.

"Susan doesn't know what she is talking about. You are Catholic and going to stay that way."

"You don't have control over my life," she screamed and left the table.

"Did Susan tell you that?"

I slumped down on the couch and continued to watch the ongoing news of people still missing.

"Can you believe her, Ralph?" He didn't say anything.

"What about you, Richard?"

"Just give her some time; I'm sure that after a few weeks she will miss the Catholic Church."

"You think so?"

"No, but maybe she will!"

"That wasn't very helpful."

"Do you think it's helpful when you say rude stuff about Susan?"

"Yes, I am aware that what I say is rude, but can you blame me?" I got up and walked through the door right after she said that.

"Virginia, do you have something to say to Susan?"

"Why don't you go up to your room? We're going to be talking about inappropriate things."

Ralph got up from the table. "Mom, how could you say that? Susan has done nothing wrong."

"She has turned Gloria away from her Catholic beliefs."

"No, Gloria has done that herself."

"Ralph, this does not involve you."

"It does when you talk bad about my friends."

He called me his friend!

"Ralph, go up to your room this instant." Then sirens started going off on the TV. The anchor said, "We have some breaking news. Everyone go down to the post office and receive a number six on your head. It is a sign that you are following Abram; if you do not have the sign on your head, you will be beheaded. You will use that number to buy everything." Virginia got up from the table.

"Mom, where are you going?"

"To get that six on my head. Now let's go, Richard. Ralph, go start the car. Gloria, get down here. Susan, get in the car with us."

"No, I will not get a six stamped on my forehead."

"You have no choice!"

"I do have a choice."

"Don't make me call the cops on you!" Gloria was already down the stairs.

"Mom, don't do it. It's okay!"

"I can't be seen with a person without a six. Now let's go." Gloria looked at the TV.

"Do I have to do this?"

"Gloria, I don't want you to die." I sat back down on the couch and turned my back. Everyone got in the car and drove to the post office.

They came back with sixes printed on their foreheads in red.

"Susan, if you are seen without a number, you will die," Gloria said as she sat down on the couch next to me.

"I'd rather die instead of go in hiding for the rest of my life."

"I'll make sure Mom does not call the police."

"Thank you, Gloria!"

She went up to her room, and so did I. I had a lot to think about. Was this going to be the end of me? Was I going to die? Was this my last stop? I had many questions that I wished could be answered. I looked in my Bible to see if this was a plague. It read, "So the first went and poured out his bowl upon the earth and a foul and loathsome sore came upon the men who had the mark of the beast and those who worshiped his image." After I read that, I felt a tingle throughout my body.

CHAPTER 27

I heard a knock at the door. Virginia answered it.

"I need to check your household members for the mark on the foreheads."

"Um, right now is not the right time," she stuttered, making it obvious that someone did not have the mark.

"Well, the time is right for us. How many are living here?"

"Five people, sir!"

"Bring all five down here!"

She stomped upstairs and into my room. "Okay, I'm sorry, but you have to come down here."

"Okay, I'm ready to meet my death."

"Wow, Gloria, Ralph, please come here." They walked into my room.

"Mom, who is at the door?"

"The police, and they have to check for the six."

"What about Susan?"

I spoke before Virginia answered. "I'll be okay. Don't worry about me. I'm not afraid of death." Virginia walked downstairs first, followed by Gloria, Ralph, Richard, and me.

"Is this all?"

"Yes sir. There is no one else."

"Check, check, check, check, and no check." He leaned in and looked at me square in the eye. "You do not have a six. Why is that?"

"I don't follow Abram; I follow the one true God."

"Take her away!" he screamed in my face. He slapped handcuffs on me.

"Susan—no, please. Is there anything else she can do?" Gloria screamed at the guard.

"Nope, Abram's orders are to kill them." A guard took me by the arms and led me outside.

"Susan—no, please. Don't take her away."

Then they closed the door. They carried me to a large truck and pushed me into the back. I rode in the back for about forty-five minutes until we reached the dome. They took me out and brought me to the middle of the dome, where I met Abram.

"Hello. I see you refuse to mark your head."

"I do!"

He nodded yes. They brought me to a platform, and they placed my head into the guillotine.

"You did refuse, so you leave me with no choice."

"I'm not afraid of death!"

"A Christian, I see! I don't like Christians."

"I know you don't."

"Why? You know who I am."

"How could I not."

"Smart one we have here."

"Smart enough to say that if you kill me, it's a straight line to paradise."

"I am smart. If I get rid of you, then I get rid of you witnessing to people."

"You may be smart, but I am smarter than you will ever be."

"I'm the only one who's going to live."

"Not for long!"

"Come now and see!" People started rushing into the stands to watch. Abram grabbed a megaphone. "Come and see. Susan Douglas does not have the mark on her head. In three, two …"

I closed my eyes and whispered, "One!"

As soon as I opened my eyes, I was standing before God and he told me, "Well done, my good and faithful child!"

Study Questions from the Author

1. What's your story? What is your spiritual background? Is it more like Susan, Amanda, Chloe, John, George…?

2. Every person in this book (expect Susan) has turned away from God somehow. How can you learn from those mistakes?

3. Susan witnessed to people in so ways. Which way can you witness to someone?

4. Susan asked Ryan, 'Do you know our Savior?' Do you?

5. John gave Susan a watch that said, '**W**alk **A**bove **T**he **C**hrist's **H**and.' What do you think that means?

6. When Susan received the medicine saying 'Only use by Susan' and John knew that; why would he take the risk?

7. When Susan arrived in New Jersey to the Richard house she called it a confused house. Why would Susan call it that?

8. Why would God let Pappy die right after he heard the gospel?

9. Susan thought this 'When you are saved, and you do sin, you feel bad and rethink about it. If you're not truly saved and you do sin, you don't feel guilty.' How does that make you feel?

10. What if the rapture happened right now? Would you be left behind or would you go see the Lord?

Acknowledgements

I t has always been a dream of mine to see my manuscript printed and bounded in a book. As I look at this miracle that I could not do on my own I thank everyone at West Bow who helped my dream come true. Without your kindness and patience I would still have a manuscript sitting in a box full of scattered dreams. Everyone that I have worked with; I pray and thank God for you for making my dream come true.

I thank my wonderful parents who invested in my dream. Mom, you have always kept me up on my feet and I thank you for all of your hard work towards me. Dad, you have always been my cheerleader. You have stood by my side and supported me 100%. I am very blessed to have wonderful, Godly parents like you two. Love you with all my heart!

No book is correct until you have right grammar. My thanks also go to Julie Boley. Thank you for your hard work that you have done to my book. Without your amazing skills, my book would be a big bowl of alphabet soup. Thank you again for your work and effort.

I want to thank the amazing talented Stephen Odum for designing the front and back cover. Thank you for spending your time on making the book come alive. I know you have worked hard on designing the cover and I thank you.

My beautiful cousin, I thank you for letting me use your face on the front cover. You are a beautiful young lady and I know God has special plans for your life. I love you with all my heart! Just remember, keep dancing!

The one thing that makes a book is words and words are hard to find. I would like to thank my pastor for finding the words to describe the Revelation. Pastor Jeff, you are my inspiration and my encourager. Thank you for being a great pastor to me and my family. You are the one who helped me find my passion and my future.

All my love goes to the God who made it all. You gave me the gift of writing and I am very blessed to be saved. You truly have made my dream come true. You have opened doors that I thought I would never walk through. Thank you Lord!

About the Author

S arah came to Christ at the age of 7 at Blackshear Place Baptist Church. After growing in her relationship with Christ she knew she had received the gift of writing.

When Sarah was 10 years old, she started her writing career. As she learned more about the second coming of Jesus Christ, she was inspired to write about it. Sarah attends C.W. Davis Middle School as an Honor Student and loves to write. Her dream was to see her writing published.

In July of 2015 Sarah got a white blue eyed Netherland Dwarf bunny. Sarah choose the name Nibbles because of her strong teeth. Nibbles sits up in the window and takes her evening naps. Sometimes when Sarah comes home from school she see's Nibbles sleeping in the window.

Visit Sarah online at canidothisalone.com
Instagram: canidothisalone

Printed in the United States
By Bookmasters